Broken on the inside

Broken on the inside

Simon Hammelburg

Aerial Media Company

ISBN 978-94-026-01008-0
NUR 301(Fiction)

© 1996, 2014 Simon Hammelburg
The moral right of Simon Hammelburg to be identified as the author of this work has been asserted in accordance with the Copyright, Designs and Patents Act of 1988.
© 2014 English edition: Aerial Media Company bv, Tiel, the Netherlands
first print

Cover design: Teo van Gerwen
Image cover: David Toms Photography, Marbella, Spain
Book design: Teo van Gerwen

www.simonhammelburg.com
www.aerialmediacom.nl
www.facebook.com/Aerialmediacompany

This book is also available as e-book: ISBN 978-94-026-0029-2

Aerial Media Company bv.
Postbus 6088
4000 HB Tiel, The Netherlands.

All rights reserved. No part of this publication may be reproduced, stored in a retrieval system, or transmitted in any form or by any means, electronic, mechanical, photocopying, recording, or otherwise, without the prior permission of both the copyright owner and the above publisher of this book.

This book may read as a novel.

However, it is based on 1200 interviews with Holocaust survivors and their children.

A list of Hebrew and Yiddish expressions and words can be found towards the back of this book on page 238 and 239.

The March of the Deceased

They are still around, they're in my head
They're still around a lot
Perhaps you can forget them
If you trust enough in God
Or when you'll rest forever
Once you die, it just may be
But all the other people
Who were saved and then set free
Will never sleep in peace
Until eternity

They're still around, they're still around
They're all over my head
They wander through my mind
Each night just as I go to bed
Before I saw the light of life
They were inside of me
The ones who didn't make it
I never got to see
They'll maybe recognize me
In eternity

They're still around, they're still alive
The pictures in my head
The camps, the dirty barracks
The fire, smell of death
My child has peaceful dreams
About the fairy tales we've read
Or when she played with grandpa
Before she went to bed
But I may only sleep after
My father gets to rest

That just may take a long time 'cause
When he puts out the light
The March of the deceased goes through
His head each night

In honor of the late Flo Kinsler.

1

Soesterberg, Holland. December.

Everything took longer that Friday. Two poorly conducted meetings in Amsterdam, overloaded schedules and people who enjoyed hearing themselves talk. Almost everyone arrived late, due to snow, hail, slippery roads, traffic jams. Trains ran far behind the regular timetable. After I finished working at ten p.m. it took me more than two hours to drive the 35 miles back home.

Coming home always generated mixed feelings of happiness and severe anxiety. I was glad to be back with Daisy and after twenty years of marriage we were still in love. However the fear that Nazis had busted the house and had taken Daisy with them, just as had happened to my parents, was still present
During the summer of 1943 the Amsterdam police force arrested my father's entire family. As a matter of coincidence he was not home. Dad had spent the night with a non-Jewish friend. In the morning he witnessed the entire Jewish neighborhood surrounded. Escorted by policemen, people marched to the tram that took them with a few belongings to the railroad station. His parents, eight brothers, his sister, uncles and aunts, he never saw again. They were all killed

in Sobibor and Auschwitz.

My mother also miraculously escaped the big razzia but silently observed how her twelve-year-old brother Henry was kicked unconscious by the policemen's leather boots, because he unsuccessfully attempted to protect his parents. They too did not return from Hitler's destruction camps. I knew it would not happen again, the world had since changed and the Nazi troops had disappeared decades ago, yet the fear stayed inside of me as a part of daily life.

As I entered the driveway I calmed down. Daisy was there, lights were on and through the closed curtains I saw that she had lit the open fire place.

Relieved I fulfilled my daily late-night obligations. I entered my office attached to the house to take a look at the mail. In the e-mail was a funny political cartoon from the New York Post. A smile sent to me by a dear friend in the United States. I glanced at the mail; mostly holiday greetings and a couple of bills. I put the flowers I bought each Friday for Daisy on my desk. I peeked around the door of the living room to check if she was still awake. The living room was peaceful and quiet. On the sofa and the coffee table were her books, magazines, a little left over wine in a glass with her lipstick on the rim. I emptied the glass, enjoying the combination of good red wine and Daisy's lipstick.

Back at the office I switched on all lights and started to prepare two urgent messages; I turned the TV on to watch the news. Only weather related stories. Ice, snow, traffic jams, accidents and hyper weathermen. They happily yelled that conditions would only get worse. Perhaps we could go ice-skating tomorrow on one of the nearby lakes?

A car stopped on our driveway. Friends down the block dropping in for a late nightcap?

Our cat jumped onto the desk to comfortably lay down beneath the desk lamp on my paperwork. She lay next to Daisy's framed picture, making sure she'd get my full attention. Her little cat brains knew that.

'What's new with you?' I asked her. 'Anything exciting? Caught any mice for me in the basement?'

Our "conversation" was interrupted by three loud bangs on the front door. As I opened the door, I saw a uniformed police officer standing in the snow, his breath steaming out of his mouth towards me.

'Can I come in for a moment?' he asked.

'Why don't you call me after the weekend to make an appointment?' I answered. I was ready to shut the door. Always the same story. My business partner Ron refused to pay his parking tickets on time.

'Your neighbors informed me that you returned home,' the police officer persisted.

I felt a great deal of anger. Were our neighbors spying on us and reporting our moves to the police, like Nazi collaborators? And was I now faced with Gestapo, banging on my door in the middle of the night, dressed in a long leather coat, wearing shiny boots?

'Call me on Monday,' I repeated.

The officer uncomfortably stared at the ground, shivering from the cold.

'I'm sorry, I can't do that sir. I would have preferred a more tactical approach but you leave me no choice. Your wife just died in a traffic accident.'

Daisy had been unexpectedly picked up by a girlfriend to join a reception. Her friend drank too much. On the way back home she had been speeding and skidded, head on into a snow plough.

'Are you sure you don't want to come in?' I now asked the police officer.

'I would have preferred to talk inside, sir. I am so sorry that it happened this way,' he answered.

'Well, thank you for coming down here in person.'

We shook hands.

On his way back to his patrol car he turned around.

'Your neighbors don't know what this is all about. I only asked them to phone me as you came home.'

He stepped into his car and drove off into the freezing night.

Daisy had been killed in a traffic accident? The message didn't sink in. Daisy was asleep in our bedroom! Her wine glass was still on the coffee table. I walked to our bedroom and switched the lights on. Our bed was empty.

On the chair were a bra and her blue skirt; her slippers were next to the bed. I could smell her favorite perfume. There was a newspaper next to her pillow. I switched the lights off and wandered back to the living room. There were no messages on the answering machine. I walked back to the office. The cat was still laying on my paperwork next to the flowers I had bought Daisy. I opened the front door again. Perhaps I had been hallucinating? The footprints of the police officer still showed in the snow along with the tire marks of his car. No doubt, he had been to our house.

I took Daisy's flowers to the kitchen and arranged them in a vase, talking out loud to myself.

'When Daisy comes home these flowers need to be on the table.'

I asked the cat if she had been fed. Just to be sure I opened a can of cat food and put it in her bowl. She purred as she started to eat.

I poured myself a large scotch and walked back to the bedroom, back to the living room and the office. Petrified, I wandered through our house. I had been planning to grab something from my desk but once there, I could not remember what. I was totally numbed and disoriented. I needed fresh air. Outside I vomited in the cold. I poured my drink onto the snow. Two yellow spots as if a dog had been urinating there.

'I need to arrange an awful lot,' I spoke to myself. Did I need to make calls or compose a list of things to do? Useless. It was 2 a.m.

Ron was to come in the morning to clean up his desk for the holidays and then we were to go visit a mutual friend together. I sat down on the sofa. The cat settled down on my lap and started purring again.

What were the last words Daisy and I exchanged after I kissed her?
'Bye, I'll see you later.'
'Be careful darling. I'll wait for you.'
Was that the end? The last words we ever exchanged, taking for granted that we would be together forever? No, I walked back in for a minute to hand her the newspaper.
'Perhaps we can go out ice-skating tomorrow afternoon. It's good for you.'
These were her last words to me.
'It's good for you.'

Ron woke me up the next morning. I had fallen asleep on the sofa, the cat on top of me. The unreal, numb feeling was still there. Over a cup of coffee we discussed what needed to be done; almost emotionless.

He started to make funeral arrangements and called Daisy's sister in Manhattan Beach, California. He quickly arranged for the necessary and cancelled the appointment with our friend.

'Let's take a break now,' I interrupted him. 'Let's go ice-skating. We won't have a chance to do that over the next few days. And, it's good for me,' I repeated Daisy's last words.

On the ice we ran into several acquaintances. We patiently listened to various complaints about back aches, mid-life crises, a man telling us that "his wife didn't understand him anymore," stress at work, depression, Prozac and a woman's hot flashes. Kids cheerfully ice-skated and threw snowballs. While on the ice we discussed the details of Daisy's funeral. A few people had to be informed by me but Ron would make most of the calls. On Saturdays Daisy and I used to be inseparable. Now I was ice-skating with Ron, preparing her funeral. What a sudden, cruel contrast. I was still unable to comprehend that she was no longer with us and that her inanimate, mutilated corpse had been temporarily stored in a drawer of a coroner's refrigerator.

As we returned home I found her weekend shopping list in the kitchen and her mail had arrived. Two bills, an invitation for a birthday party and a personalized pocket diary from a credit card company. The covetous banker posthumously wished her a 'Happy New Year.'

A salesperson called.

'Hi, how are you doing today sir.'

'I am fine, thank you.'

'May I talk to Daisy please?'

'She can only be reached long distance,' I answered.

'Do you have a number for me sir?'

'No, I don't. It's an unlisted number, as far as I know.'

'Could you ask her to let me know when she is back in town?'

'You'll be the first to know.'

'Thanks, I really appreciate it sir. Just tell her to ask for Mary at the Yellow Pages.'

Our office assistant, Meta, arrived with take-out lunches. It was almost three o'clock and we had not even thought about eating.

'I'll make sure that you won't get any visitors prior to the funeral,' she said. 'I will seal you off from the outside world and protect you like a lion.'

As she started to work, she swallowed her tears. She and Daisy had been best friends.

The first phone call that I made was to Benny in New York. He would have to alter his itinerary. He had been planning on coming to stay with us for a few days and spend a long weekend together with Daisy in Paris.

I thought that this would be an easy call. We had known each other for over twenty years. We were with him when his wife died of cancer. He had told me his personal history, so I was under the impression that he was the ultimate expert in coming to terms with losing family members.

In 1939 he escaped Nazi Germany. He tried to get from Berlin to Holland but was stopped by the Dutch border police and handed over to their German counterparts. He still had the old passport. On page eight there was a red stamp: "Refused, Border Police Zevenaar." That was like a death sentence.

Somehow he managed to escape his guards and make it to Hamburg, where he boarded a ship that sailed via Rotterdam to South America. He left behind all of his family, his seventeen-year-old fiancée Frieda, friends and most of his belongings.

Upon arrival in Montevideo, Uruguay, he arranged for Frieda's escape, spending his last money on corrupt diplomats who arranged for a "proxy wedding." Based on a law on family reunion, the Uruguayan government provided her with a visa. Frieda escaped

Hitler's destruction plans on the last vessel that had permission to leave for South America.

After the war they relocated to New York. He became a successful pediatrician, she an anesthesiologist. Together they raised three children in their home in New Rochelle. None of his family members survived the Holocaust. He never found out where and how they were killed.

With a big smile, he once proudly showed me a book he had borrowed from the Jewish Library in Berlin.

'We hardly got the chance to get outside,' he explained. 'So I read a lot. Thus I asked for two books. But that was against the rules. One book a day'. Ironically this took place in the morning prior to the Kristallnacht in November 1938. The next morning all Jewish businesses, offices and synagogues had been looted, destroyed or set on fire; including the library. 'I should return it,' he said. 'But to whom?'

After Frieda passed away, he spent much of his time with us. He took Daisy to places he and Frieda used to go. Talking about personal losses, I was sure that I was calling a veteran expert with whom I could share sadness.

Yet his response was subdued.

'I am so sorry to hear that,' he said. 'I know all about it. But, as is written in the Talmud: If one door closes, another one will open. Meanwhile you must use the old medicine, keep the stiff upper lip.'

The second long distance call I made was to my brother Eric. He, his wife and two children also lived in the suburbs of New York.

'If there is anything I can do, let me know,' he offered.

It sounded like an empty offer, but well meant.

His wife came on the phone too.

'It's strange,' she said. 'I didn't really know her that well after all these years. You two always maintained such a secluded private life. I wouldn't actually know what she was really like.'
For a moment I searched for words. How could you describe your own wife in a few words?
'She meant the world to me,' I answered.
'Oh, yes, that tells me a lot about her,' my sister-in-law responded. 'Okay, I guess we have different lifestyles and I don't understand yours.'
After I finished that conversation I asked Meta: 'Would you be capable of describing Daisy in a few words?'
She frowned her brow.
'Ask the wrong question and you'll get the wrong answer,' she responded.

The neighbors, who had been kind enough to call the police the night before, received me with open arms, coffee and cake.
'Oh my God,' the woman kept repeating after learning of what had happened; she blubbered in a wrinkled hanky.
Her husband, an insurance agent who always gave us unwanted advice, wanted to know in detail how Daisy had crashed and died. He listened, shaking his head and then asked me if she had life insurance.
'I told you so,' he responded after I told him that the answer was negative.
'At least you would have had some financial compensation. Not that it can replace a human being, but you would have had something. Now you have nothing at all.'
I politely thanked him for his moral support.

As I walked back into my office, Ron and Meta had finalized all details for the funeral.

When I wanted to ask some questions, Meta promptly interrupted me..

'I don't suppose you are interested in the specifics of the design of the coffin,' she said. 'It is sickening but they have a whole variety, a catalogue with numerous options for the interior as if we are decorating a new bedroom. Only more expensive.'

'Whatever you do is fine,' I said. 'No one has ever returned to complain about the lack of luxury or comfort in a coffin, I guess.'

We decided to grab a bite at a local Chinese joint.

'Your wife isn't coming tonight?' our regular waitress asked with her friendly smile.

Upon leaving she gave me some take-out goodies.

'For your wife,' she said. 'Don't eat them yourself. Next time I will check with her to see if you gave them to her.'

'Don't you forget,' I answered.

No one said a word as we walked back home through the ice cold winter night.

2

Over two hundred people attended the funeral. I recognized many faces. Some of them greeted me with their eyes or a gesture with their hands, some avoided eye contact. They did not know how to react and I couldn't blame them. I was glad they were there.

'Some of us believe in God, others don't,' I heard the rabbi preach at Daisy's grave.
'In both cases we don't have to worry about the deceased anymore. If there is an Almighty, she is now in a better world, without pain, hurt or sadness and she will be waiting for us to join her. If there is no God we don't have to worry either. In that case there is nothing she can feel anymore. She doesn't suffer. So we must not worry about her. The emotions, the sadness are within ourselves and we have to learn how to cope with the harsh reality.'
Minutes later he asked me if he had done a good job. I listened to the sound of the shovels of dirt plump down on Daisy's coffin.
'At least you didn't proclaim that it was God's will,' I answered him.
'I understand,' was his response. 'But the fact that I didn't bring it up must have been God's will. You know that I have an answer to everything. That comes with the profession.'
He smiled at me. We had known each other since early childhood.

The guests escaped the freezing cold and went into the community hall of the local synagogue to offer their condolences, cry, drink coffee and eat cake.

'Their appetite is good,' Meta joked.

'It's a bloody shame,' my mother complained loudly so everybody could hear. 'This cake is at least three days old. It's beyond me that they have the nerve to charge you a fortune and serve weak coffee and old cake. They should be ashamed. But they are never ashamed. When they are collecting money they act so courteous. But when you need anything in return, this is what you get.'

'I am sorry, my sweet Daisy,' I whispered. 'Your funeral was tasteful, during the reception I heard two new jokes, but the quality of the cake was subject to discussion. Let's say, the cake was questionable, next time better.'

My mother put her heavy arms around my neck. A load of make-up was dripping down in tears onto my shirt.

'My child,' she screamed. 'You have no idea how much you are hurting me. You are my own flesh and blood. I am your mother. So when you are hurt, I hurt even more. I know how it feels when your family dies, or worse, to watch them being killed in front of my own eyes. Do you know how these bastards kicked my little brother down the stairs? The sweetheart. He was too good for this world.'

Yes, I knew, but I kept silent. There was a long line of guests waiting for her to move forward or step aside so we could shake hands. My mother did not seem to be aware of that.

'Those bastards called my mother a slut. She was such a darling. They molested my brother, like you wouldn't even do to an animal. Such a sweet boy. Maybe nobody in this room knows what you are going through, but I do, because I am your mother and you only have one mother in your life.'

'Thanks God,' I whispered in her ear, 'Just one mother!'
She didn't hear me and burst into tears, like a tropical rain storm.
'I can't take this anymore,' she screamed. 'I am going to faint.'
My father determinedly pushed her aside.
'What else is new?' he said. 'You know her. She never listens. Everything goes in one ear and out the other. She was born without a receiver. She only has a transmitter and that never stops. The other day she wanted to show me a new "magical trick" that she had learned. I said "okay, please quietly disappear." She didn't even pick that up. I can say whatever I want. She recently asked me if I had paid my fees to the Jewish Community, so we can be buried at a Jewish cemetery. "For you I paid twice, because you need a Californian king size grave," I said. She didn't hear that one either. Did you already make plans on what you are going to do next?'
'I haven't had time to even think about it.'
'You should have. Just sitting home, whining won't do you any good. May I ask you a personal question? Are you having an affair with Meta? Your mother doesn't think so, but I do. Meta is such an open-minded, intelligent woman. Don't get me wrong, I sort of liked Daisy, but you have to admit that she wasn't the right wife for you, and a dud of a housewife. I warned you back then, but you refused to listen. That's the destructive nature of your character. You always choose the wrong friends and partners. Now you are being confronted with your own blunders and you're alone again.'
'Are you blaming Daisy for dying on me?' I asked indignantly.
'To a certain extent, yes. She was irresponsible, driving under the influence. That's asking for trouble. Well, I'll see you later at home.'
Before I could say that I didn't yet want any visitors at home that day, he turned his back on me and walked away, making space for the other guests. There were many nice consolatory words and gestures.

They kept me going.

When the reception was finished I was exhausted and glad that it was all over. I enjoyed a short time of silence and privacy while driving home. That did not take long though.
My parents had invited themselves to my home.
My mother had demarcated the kitchen as her territory.
'She was a good person,' she mumbled, 'but a sloppy housewife. Look at this. I am amazed that she was able to find anything in this mess.' While criticizing Daisy she started to reorganize and clean the cupboards and drawers.
My father was not content with the funeral service.
'That rabbi friend of yours is a bit of a humbug,' he complained. 'He was your choice, right? I am quite tolerant and understanding, but this man doesn't know anything about Judaism. Even your mother noticed, that's how bad it was.'
I no longer followed his monologue. In my head I still heard the sound of the shovels of dirt plump down on Daisy's coffin. I recalled the expressions on the faces of the guests at the funeral and some of their endearing words. I was anxiously wondering how to get through the coming night.
I watched my father's reprehensible facial expressions, thought of my sister-in-law's remarks. "I really didn't know her that well," or something like that.
Not a fair statement. She had never taken the effort or shown any interest. Not knowing someone is something else. I never had a chance to know my grandparents, uncles, aunts or their children. I had been unable to touch them, hear their voices, or sense a smell. Like a big, black hole. My parents unsuccessfully tried to tell me about them. They used their entire vocabulary, which was

insufficient to describe a vanished world. A vicious circle. The more they tried, the less I heard and the louder they talked about the cruel details of death and destruction. People and their homes I had never seen and would never get the chance to see. My sister-in-law had the chance to get to know Daisy but simply wasn't interested. That's a big difference.

My parents, my brother and I had never been like a real family. Each one lived in his own world, with different thoughts, opinions and memories. Father and mother formed a couple without a foundation. Two childhood acquaintances who met again in 1945 at a Red Cross office where long lists of the dead from the Holocaust covered the walls. Neither of them found a single person who escaped the Nazis madness. Coincidence created the mismatch between them, not love. Compulsion kept them together.

From early childhood my mother had been vomiting her distorted memories over us. It smelled like death. She was an hysterical, insatiable woman with severe mood changes. A kiss and a hug could suddenly, unexpectedly turn into physical and verbal violence. You could see the madness in her eyes.

My father withdrew into his own small world. He did not talk much, but had a negative judgment on everything and everybody. He did not greet his neighbors. He called them "barbaric crooks, wealthy textile Jews without an appropriate background or manners."

Children were little inferior adults to him. They had to learn, work and be able to discuss the Talmud over dinner. There was no space for emotions. He never touched us. Only after we were adults we sometimes shook hands.

Once he caught me reading a children's book, a gift from a neighbor. He took it from me and snapped: 'You don't learn anything reading this nonsense.'

He gave me another book. 'Here is something educational.'

It was a book about the uprising and extermination of the Warsaw ghetto.

'This will teach you about mankind. There are just a few heroes in this world where nobody can be trusted, unless when they promise to kill you. Then they'll keep their word.'

My brother was sent away from home when he was eight. My parents had decided that "he was good for nothing" and had no future prospects.

My parents' decision was triggered by an incident at school. He had failed a test because he had not done his homework. He was supposed to show the paper, for which he received a D+, to my father and the teacher had required his signature. To avoid the predictable consequences, my brother forged my father's signature, which was obvious to the teacher.

From my bedroom I listened in to the conversation that lead to my parents' *final solution*.

'My son is a swindler, a crook. I cannot tolerate that in my house,' I heard my father argue.

My mother tried to defend him, but that only made things worse.

'Maybe he inherited these manners from your side of the family, certainly not from me,' he groused to my mother.

Then came the verdict. My brother was sent to a very strict boarding school with a rigid regime, far away from home in a remote village.

'Hopefully there they'll teach him some manners,' my father said. 'I can't keep up with that child of yours.'

My mother became hysterical. I was furious, jumped out of my bed and yelled at my father: 'You are going to deport him. You are just like a Nazi who decides whom will be on the next transport.'

He completely ignored me for over a year.

He met my brother just once more. After a long evaluation my brother decided to introduce his fiancée to my father. He came down like a sledge hammer.

'If you choose to destroy your life with this monstrosity, go right ahead, but don't ask for my blessing. I am not blessing a certain disaster to happen to my own son. Once your adolescent obsessions calm down you are going to be bored to tears with this brainless Barbie.'

Eric's last attempt was to talk him into lending him the equivalent of forty dollars, so he could buy a suit for the wedding.

'Apparently you feel old enough to make your own stupid decisions. So act like an adult and pay your own bills. You have cost me enough already. First you refused to learn, then to work. You are unable to love your family in a normal manner, so you are a sociopath.'

They never talked again and my parents never saw their two grandchildren. A severe self-punishment for a dispute over a forty dollar loan.

I looked at my father's face and noticed that he hadn't changed a bit in all these years.

A knock on my door interrupted my thoughts. It was the rabbi who came to ask if I was all right or needed anything.

'If you need me, you know where to find me,' he offered. 'You may come or call no matter what time of the day or night.'

My father gave him a grumpy look, ordered my mother to put her coat on and left without saying a word. He paid his respects, in his remarkable way and I didn't need a dictionary. He did his best.

As I watched them drive into the street, I tried to get a picture of the house where he grew up. Nothing came to mind. My perspective of time seemed to have disappeared. Here I was, unsure about the future. In the far past there was nothing. Only the dead. The only realistic memories were of a destroyed childhood, years of verbal and physical abuse by my parents. I was unable to objectively recollect the recent past with Daisy. Endearing, precious memories, created only sadness now. The end of the only happy era in my life turned to dust.

How can a person go on without happy memories? I was desperate. "Maybe, if the past hurts too much, you should create a new one," I thought. That would mean starting all over, carrying myself into the future for a while and try to remember everything pleasurable that happened. A hard task. I even had difficulties recalling what had happened over the past few days.

After the rabbi left I sat down behind my desk. I made a few notes of what had happened on that cold night when the police officer brought me the bad news. In front of me there was an almost empty notebook and a small photo camera that Daisy recently bought me. I was determined to take notes every day and to photograph people I would meet. Maybe, just maybe, I could share the pictures and new memories with myself someday. A new notebook and a brand new camera to hold on to.

That evening Daisy's sister called from Manhattan Beach. She and her husband apparently had been out of town, so Ron had left them a message on their answering machine. After I brought her up to date she hardly reacted. Instead she told me a lengthy story about a golf tournament they had just returned from. Her husband's employer invited his employees and their spouses once a year to hit a few balls and socialize during a long weekend. This year they had been to Monterey and it had been "terrific, awesome, cool," amongst a few other superlatives.

Her husband asked if Daisy had left a will and if so, if his wife was beneficiary.

'I am not sure,' I answered. 'But I will put you in mine. I will leave you my Schiller collection in Gothic German.'

'Okay,' he said. 'I hate to do this, but I have to let you go because we have been invited to a barbecue. Take good care of yourself now.'

3

During the shiva, a week of mourning, I felt like a guest in my own house. People walked in and out; some in an attempt to cheer me up, others modestly showed their sympathy. The latest jokes circulated and people cried. In some miraculous way there was always plenty of food. The kitchen was constantly used, the coffee pot could not been emptied and the coffee table was overloaded with delicious snacks.

There were still phone calls for Daisy. Her garage informed us that is was time for an oil change and tune-up. The local dry cleaner returned two skirts, an evening dress and her favorite silk scarf. A giant turkey was delivered for a surprise dinner party I didn't know about. I had no clue as to who had been invited.

The police officer who had informed me about the accident, late Friday night, delivered Daisy's belongings that were found on her in the wreck of the car and at the crash site. I left the large padded envelope unopened, avoiding a confrontation with her belongings covered in dirt and blood.

An elderly affectionate couple stopped by. Ted and Rivka. I had no idea who they were or why they came. They lived in a nursing home in Israel, were on a short vacation in Holland and after reading Daisy's obituary in a newspaper, they had spontaneously decided to come visit.

The man, Ted, had been a friend of my uncle Samuel, one of my father's brothers, killed in Sobibor.

'I knew your grandfather too,' he told me. 'A remarkable rabbi. His work was of great importance. The entire community respected him. But Samuel and he did not get along too well I think. You see, your grandfather was a devoted scholarly recluse. He didn't spend much time with his family. Your grandmother couldn't manage such a large family on her own. The children looked like starvelings. Your deceased grandmother and her only daughter walked around in old rags. They must have lived in deep poverty, but there were thousands of Hebrew books and you know what? There wasn't one toy around. The children didn't even have tooth brushes. Samuel couldn't stand that atmosphere and I couldn't blame him. Having fun or playing was outlawed at home. The only social talk during dinner, were serious conversations on who had learned what on Judaism that day. Your grandfather would ask questions, as if he was giving them the first degree. He always corrected them, putting them down. But that was not the only reason that the kids didn't like dinnertime. Your grandmother was the worst cook in the neighborhood. Everything was tasteless and chewy. No surprise that the children were suffering from stomach aches.

Your uncle Sammy was the black sheep. He loved to go dance, was full of jokes and always had gorgeous girlfriends. When he announced that he was going to study philosophy, all hell broke loose. I believe that your uncle made that choice on purpose. Philosophy contradicts fundamentalism. Your grandfather expected him to follow in his footsteps and didn't tolerate disobedience. Sammy was kicked out of his home without a penny in his pocket. He had nowhere to go so he moved in with me. For several months we shared my room. We became close friends. He was a strong, humorous man, who kept his morale high, even after we were forced into hiding and later in the transportation camp of Westerbork, the Dutch hallway to Auschwitz and Sobibor.'

His wife Rivka interrupted him.

'I don't think this is the right occasion to go into that Ted.'

Ted ignored her.

'Life in Westerbork was hard, you understand? Some people stayed for just a short period of time. Others stayed quite a while. It was a matter of luck, inventiveness, connections or coincidence. You knew that you had to stay off the deportation list of the feared train that left each Tuesday to the death camps. Once you were on that train eastwards, there was no return. However, the destination sign on the train showed Westerbork-Auschwitz and vice versa. As if you were travelling on a round trip. But we knew that we would not return on these trains to the camps.

I know of only one man who managed to stay until the end of the war. He is still a friend of mine. He had protection from the mistress of camp commander Gemmeker, because he used his artistic skills to make glorified drawings of the commander and his mistress, who was the most feared creature in the camp. He made many drawings there. Drawing was actually strictly forbidden, but he had the protection of the camp commander's mistress. He was lucky, or maybe not. While trying to survive himself he witnessed over sixty of his family members being deported to the destruction camps, unable to rescue a single one of his beloved. I met him yesterday. Still going strong but a nervous wreck. He never talked about camp Westerbork until recently. Now he doesn't stop. He described several times how he saw all of his family march to the train to the death camps. His daughter, she must be in her sixties now, broke down, interrupting her career. When he told that story repeatedly to her he didn't realize that he talked about her grandparents, aunts and uncles too. He also transferred all of his anxieties to her. First by maintaining silence, then by nervously repeating his sufferings. These things unfortunately happen.

Circumstances in Westerbork were miserable. We had to work in rain and mud in what was left of our clothes, not to mention our shoes. Families were separated, we had to share a crib with two others, food was rationed and awful, but we knew anything was better than being put on that train. The road to the station was called "Le Boulevard des Misères." Even children, the sick and demented were thrown into the cattle-wagons. There was one small barrel. A toilet. Can you imagine how filthy it became? Later I learned that 93 trains left Westerbork for the death camps, transporting over a hundred thousand Jews. The Camp Commander lied after the war that he had no knowledge of the destruction in the concentration camps and where the trains went. He was sentenced to only ten years in prison, but got out after serving just six. Unbelievable. He received a letter with compliments about his work from Adolf Eichmann, who oversaw the destruction of the Jews for Hitler. Most Dutch Jews were arrested by Dutch Police. The deportation camp was guarded on the outside by Dutch Military Police. Many of the Jews were betrayed because the Nazis paid a small amount of cash for each Jew reported to them. Anne Frank was sold for 6 or 8 German Marks I believe. The amount was raised periodically, to report a Jew in hiding. The Dutch Railroad Cooperation, like in other countries, were reimbursed by the Nazis for the one way tickets. Sammy was one of the few who kept his good spirit. He never complained, still came up with new jokes, and made connections with the other prisoners who were in charge of composing the weekly deportation list. Sometimes he was instrumental in keeping people off that list for a while. Of course others were sent instead, but there was no choice, you see? He felt very guilty about it. He had connections with a resistance group outside the camp. Once he falsified paperwork. He put names on the transportation list of nineteen men, as if they had been deported and helped them escape.

Some of them were arrested, but most of them made it, I heard. Samuel organized cultural events in the midst of all this. Prisoners acted in plays. You won't believe it but we were actually having fun, even about the Nazis. There were these two great men; Max and Nol. They called themselves Johnny and Jones. They sang funny songs, partly in Dutch, partly in English, until English was outlawed. They continued in German. Still they were joking about the supervisor's slave labor barracks where they had to take airplane wrecks apart that were shot down. I remember them as heroes, because they made children laugh and forget their misery for a few hours.

Of course, one day their names were on the deportation list. Like so many others they disappeared and left us in emptiness. My neighbor in our nursing home happened to be in the same cattle-wagon. He escaped by jumping off the train. Someone else told him that the boys were sick upon arrival in Poland. Some sort of diarrhea. It happened to all of us, sooner or later. But their timing was bad in a place where there was no space for the sick. They, or one of them, were thrown out of their barracks in the freezing cold and were found dead the next morning. I don't know for sure, but that's what my neighbor says.

Your uncle Samuel was transported a week later. I have never talked to anyone who has seen him since. Killed upon arrival I guess. He was a great person. That's why I wanted to meet with you.'

His wife Rivka interrupted him, successfully this time.

'He always talks too much when the issue comes up.'

'I know,' said Ted. 'But you see, I thought perhaps you were interested. Maybe it was not the appropriate moment, but I don't know if we'll get a chance to meet again. We are getting old, you know? Travelling becomes increasingly more difficult.'

Ted and Rivka were ready to leave.

'Before I let you go, did Samuel tell you much about his brothers and sister?' I asked.

'Strangely enough no,' Ted responded. 'He really resented that ultra-orthodox family. He used to make cynical jokes about his mother being constantly pregnant and the size of the family. But no, he never told me what was in the back of his mind. Not even when we were roommates. My recollection about these other children is poor. But, in case you are interested, I can give you the address of a boy who lived in the house where we were in hiding. Maybe he remembers? Listen to me? Boy I say. He must be an old man by now. I always send him a New Year's card. He used to bring us food and books. Samuel gave him his watch. That was the only way that we could show our appreciation for all his kindness.'

Before Ted left he wrote down the address of Horst Sachsse, whose parents apparently hid Jews, including my uncle Sammy.

4

I met Horst Sachsse and his wife Ursula almost a year later when I was in Los Angeles. They lived in a small house on the wrong side of the tracks in Encenitas, next to a noisy freeway. Before I rang the doorbell I peeked through a small window in the front door. There was a gigantic Christmas tree with hundreds of ornaments and flashing lights. The walls were covered with cuckoo clocks, deer, and wild pig heads. A German house in California. When Horst opened the door he was overly excited.

'Come see, Frau,' he shouted. 'Come now, what is taking you so long? Look who is here. This is the relative of these Jews who lived in our basement. Would you like some *schnapps* or a piece of homemade pie?'

'No thank you, I'm fine,' I answered.

'You have to eat and drink something,' he protested. 'You've come all the way down here to see us.'

He poured me a shot of *schnapps*.

Ursula served big pieces of chocolate cake.

'Fresh from my oven. I baked it this morning,' she explained.

Before I had a chance to take a bite they insisted on showing me their house. The spic-and-span kitchen with colorful typically German drapes and wallpaper, the hobby room where Horst fixed his clocks, their bedroom that looked like a hotel room in Bavaria and a shelf with framed black and white, faded photographs of people I could hardly distinguish.

'There is not too much left of the past,' Horst explained. 'Most of it got stolen or lost.'

'Your parents must have been heroes,' I said.

Horst started to laugh.

'Heroes, oh no, not at all. Ursula, you know. We were an average Christian family in Tempelberg near Berlin. My parents were not involved with the resistance at all. My father made candies, downstairs from where we lived. I was his delivery boy. Every day after school I went out with my barrow. One day I returned and saw SS and SA (Assault Division) officers looting our outlet. My father was arrested and shot dead. Being a small child I didn't understand why they were doing this. My parents never talked politics at home. To be frank, I didn't even know what a Jew was. Later my mother told me that my dad had been supporting a Jewish family. The man was a former employee that my dad had been forced to fire because he was Jewish. A new Nazi law. He gave him a little bit of money and food every week. One of the neighbors must have noticed that he came to see my father once a week and reported him to the police. Sharing, as we were taught in church, suddenly was a crime which he paid for with his life.'

Horst paused for a minute, on the verge of tears, digesting the pictures of the past.

'What happened to you and your mother?' I asked him.

'We fled to Amsterdam. Mother had a couple of friends there, where we could stay in safety. A typical old Amsterdam house with steep stairs.

It was only after we moved in that we discovered the neighbors below us were hiding people in our joint basement. They were not very nice to these people. The man was openly anti-Semitic. The Minister at their church had ordered him to help. He obeyed with a lot of aversion. He constantly made insulting remarks and did not take proper care of them. At that time in Amsterdam there was a cynical Jewish slogan about anti-Semites who reluctantly hid Jews, because their priests told them, "You Nazis, keep your filthy paws off our fucking Jews!"

My mother provided them with some food, books and clean laundry. At the time I didn't really know what exactly was going on. I was just a little boy, you see? It was safer that I didn't know. At some point police searched the house. The two in hiding were arrested along with the neighbors and my mother, betrayed by someone down the street. My mother was a pretty woman who - of course - spoke German fluently. She pretended she was flirting with a German officer, told him a few jokes so he let her go. She told me later how the two men in the basement had been suffering and how they had been constantly humiliated by their temporary rescuers. They must have gone through hell. God knows what happened to them.'

I asked him about my uncle Samuel.

'I really don't remember too much,' he answered. 'One of them is still alive. He still sends me New Year's cards from Israel. Is he your uncle?'

I shook my head. 'No, he isn't.'

'I didn't know their names, you know. I only saw them briefly to bring them some food. I was not supposed to talk to them but of course I did. They were nice people. One of them often hugged me. He was funny. He always told me a few jokes. Where he got them from in that basement puzzled me. He gave me his watch as a present. It's still running because I can repair it myself. I wear it each year on Memorial Day.

As a child I was afraid that I would go to hell if I didn't help them, and that I would go to hell too if I ignored my mother's instructions to minimize contact with them. Oh well, it's all so long ago. We are so glad you came. It is the nicest Christmas present I could have wished for, don't you think, Frau?'

I took a picture of Horst and Ursula in front of their giant Christmas tree. Ursula gave me a large bouquet from her own greenhouse. They were waving vigorously as I drove into the dark night. A German couple in America. He was an uprooted man who had shared some memories with me, seen through the eyes of a little child, a child that I liked. Horst knew that.

Horst reminded me of my early childhood neighbor Ludo. He was a few years older than me. He hardly ever played outside, not even during weekends. During school vacations he stayed with his father in Germany. We sometimes communicated through a closed window. My parents did not allow me to talk to him.

Once I came home with a chocolate bar, a reward for picking up some groceries for Ludo's mother. My mother walked, as usual, half naked through our slovenly house. She hugged me to her unpalatable body, which nauseated me. Especially her smell.

When I proudly told her that I had "earned" a chocolate bar from Ludo's mother, she was struck by an hysterical attack.

'You accepted that from that slut?' she yelled. 'That dirty Nazi whore?'

Angry and out of control she stomped into the kitchen and came back, carrying a steaming pan with our evening food.

'Never ever talk to that bitch or that little Nazi-bastard of hers again,' she yelled.

'When we had no food, madam was partying with her SS-lover. Throwing parties with champagne and caviar, baking cakes using three eggs. We were starving but she wouldn't even give us old, leftover bread. She fed that to the birds.'

Her eyes radiated a terrifying anger. She started to shake and dropped the pan on the floor, spilling a mixture of mashed potatoes and gravy on the rug.

'Look, that's what you make me do,' she yelled as she slapped me in the face.

'Now are you going to clean it up too? Well are you?'

She grabbed my hair and pushed my head into the steaming food.

'Even when I push your nose into it you don't appreciate food. Do you?'

The yelling became louder.

In my struggle to keep breathing, I didn't notice that my face got burned. That, I only realized later.

She burst into tears and pulled my head up. With a spoon she started to scrape a combination of food and dust from the floor and forced the spoon into my mouth.

'Eat or I'll make you eat,' she screamed in tears. 'I would have been all too happy with this food while that bitch was partying. Even if I had to eat it off the floor. I did not make ugly faces like you are doing. I was grateful, but of course you don't understand because we spoil you too much.'

Again she tried to force the spoon into my mouth.

'I'm not hungry,' I tried.

'You are not what? Mister smartass is not what? You won't even eat when I feed you? You don't even know how hunger feels. We didn't mind that there was mold on the bread. We fought for a slice. It tasted awful, but we were thankful to have something in our stomachs.

The hunger was terrible. Especially when it was freezing cold and we couldn't use a heater. You cannot imagine how that feels. Or can you? Maybe it would be a good lesson for you to be exposed to it for a while. Perhaps then you'd learn to appreciate the way your father and I are spoiling you.'

A neighbor, alarmed by the noise, knocked on the door to ask what was going on.

'Mind your own business, you filthy collaborator,' she screamed at him. 'Get lost.'

She grabbed me by the ear and yelled, 'Now you see what you are doing to me? You make a fool of me in front of my own neighbors. Are you proud of yourself? Look at me. Food all over the floor, neighbors knocking on my door. I can't keep up with you anymore. I will call the police and have you arrested, so you can spend your life in prison with your fellow scumbags. You are a sadist. You inherited that from your father's family. Dirty sadists.'

All of a sudden her mood changed.

'I wish you had known my parents,' she whispered with a smile, tears still on her cheeks. 'They were such darlings. My dad, rest his soul, my dad used to put my mother in a big rocking chair and bring her flowers whenever she was in a bad mood. Then he said in Yiddish, "Merele, let me bring a homage to you." Every day he laced her shoes for her. On his knees. And you know what these policemen did? They arrested him. Like a criminal. They killed him in the gas chamber. Meanwhile, madam the whore, the same one you like to go shopping for in exchange for a chocolate bar, got laid by her Gunter. After the liberation we shaved her head, so everyone noticed that she had been a Nazi whore, but that was not half of what she deserved.'

My father came home and matter-of-factly asked what was going on.

'That beastly child of yours is impossible again. He drives me crazy. We should lock him up in a psychiatric institution. Maybe they can handle him there.'

My father sent me to my room. Through the wall I listened to them arguing. All their conversations sounded like arguments. She loud, with a piercing voice, he remained calm. Usually she was crying as they talked. That infuriated him. I could not hear exactly what they were talking about. Only a few words.

'You have no idea what that child..., the police will..., you never do...' The familiar background music in my bedroom. I crawled underneath my bed. Hiding in my own "safe house," protecting myself from violence and chaos. I had everything I needed. A flashlight, books. An apple or an orange that the owner of the grocery store would give to me, or a roll from the bakery on the corner.

The bed was my roof. Never ever did I want to lie on that bed again. It was my worst enemy.

One late night I called my mother, after a nightmare. I didn't realize that she was in an angry mood.

She smashed my bedroom door open, took a few angry steps and then tripped over one of my shoes. Her full three hundred pounds collapsed on the wooden floor that almost gave way under her weight. She screamed as I never heard before. She switched the light on. She grabbed me by the neck and pushed my nose onto her shinbone. There was a dark blue bruise, smelling like pus.

'See what you have done now,' she yelled. 'You've crippled me. You've crippled your own mother.'

Later I learned that the policemen who arrested her parents kicked her on the leg, so hard and so long that she could see the bone underneath. One of the wounds that would never heal.

She became so furious with me that she grabbed me by the arm and pulled me to the kitchen, dislocating my elbow. She smashed my head into an open cupboard where the cat's litter box was. I could see crawling vermin and smell the litter box that had not been cleaned for ages. Cat stools were all over my face. The impact broke the ceramic litter box. The sharp edge cut my breast, like a razor blade. I jumped up and ran to my bedroom. I tried to move my hand and fingers. My wrist was broken. My hand had twisted ninety degrees and swollen.

I sat on my bed for hours, shivering in pain, afraid to make a sound that would only make things worse. I hoped for my father to come in, but had to wait until the morning.

'Nonsense,' he calmly spoke. 'There is nothing wrong with you. You just try to make your own mother look ridiculous. She already has so many guilty feelings. If you keep that attitude, crying over nothing, we may not notice when something is really the matter. When I was a child I could be sick for ten days. No one even noticed. My mother lost track of the number of children, my father was too busy studying the Talmud. Chin up, I'll help you get dressed and then it's off to school.'

A few hours later my school teacher sent me home, to go see a doctor. 'If you force me to take you to a doctor, I will,' my mother sighed. 'But not like this. You haven't washed, you're disgusting and you smell. Look how dirty your fingernails are. I will be ashamed of myself if you show up dirty like this at the doctor's office. You are not going to make me look foolish, because you refuse to wash yourself properly.' She grabbed my broken wrist and pulled me into the bathroom, took a big scrubber, a jar of soft soap and started to brush my fingernails, engulfing me in pain. When I was finally brought into the emergency room, my fingernails were shinier than ever.

Shortly afterward, I built my little home underneath my bed. Only the cat was allowed into my shelter.

I never talked to Ludo or his mother again. Ludo left for good to live with his father in Germany. His mother moved to another neighborhood where her reputation was undamaged.

5

The week after Daisy's funeral passed by like a chaotic dream. An open house. Some people visited every day, others just once, to offer their condolences. My house looked like a coffee shop, a meeting place for people who hadn't seen each other for a while.

I had not seen my father since the day of the funeral. My mother acted like a jamming station, because she had taken the opportunity to "reorganize" my house, as she called it.

'If you are not organized you create a muddle,' she had informed us. She gave a long list of instructions to the housekeeper. I told her to ignore them, which she did. Without complaining she let my mother interfere with her work and politely ignored her instructions and critical remarks.

'I don't know what possessed Daisy,' my mother complained. 'Everyone knows that you shouldn't keep eggs in the refrigerator. They absorb the odors of the other food. And bacteria. That causes salmonella. Don't look surprised now. A lady friend of mine almost died of it. That's because that dullard doctor of ours misdiagnosed. That's his hobby. When I was young, you had to be an intelligent person to attend university and from a good family too. Nowadays they accept all kinds of mental defects, so you have to rely on some young unsophisticated quack. I phoned this new, so called doctor, when I had bronchitis. You think that these kids still make house calls? Forget it. In the pouring rain I had to come to his office. I thought that I was going to die. I have weak lungs, you know, since the war. It's a miracle that I am still alive. You know what he told me? That it was a simple cold. Told me to eat an orange every day and take vitamins. That did it. When I told your father, he checked with his medical encyclopedia. And you know what? I had been right all the time. I was suffering from serious bronchitis. Fortunately I had some medication that the old doctor had prescribed, God have his soul, so I took that and sure enough it helped. Had I listened to that kid I might have died. I can still feel it.'

Proving her point she started to breathe fast and very deep, producing a squeaking sound that everyone in the house could hear.

'Oh my God, now I am dizzy again. What are you doing?' she chastised the housekeeper. 'You are not going to tell me that you put the good china in the dishwasher? I don't believe it.'

She took all the plates, cups and glasses the housekeeper had just put in the dishwasher out and put them in the sink.

'Just hand wash them, or is that too much to ask? And careful, otherwise they get chipped.'

My brother frequently called, but we were unable to really communicate.
'What are you doing all day long?'
'I talk to people. They are having a good time. I serve them food and drinks. It's just like a cozy pub. You should come join us.'
'I am much too busy. You have no idea. Tons of work. Hold on, there is someone on the other line... Yes, that's me again. It's a madhouse here. Tomorrow I have to travel to Holland for a lawsuit.'
'While you're in Holland, come visit.'

'No way. You know, I have such a heavy schedule. Perhaps I'll take a few friends to dinner, but that is all. Besides, I am not in the mood for small talk at your place full of visitors. It's a waste of time. For you too. Get on with your life, back to work. That's healthier than all that emotional crap.'

'I'm not sure,' I answered. 'Perhaps I should adjust my life somehow. Just continuing what I was doing seems like taking a step back into the past.'

'I don't understand a word of what you say,' he responded. 'I have to go now. Do whatever you like. It's your life. Say hello for me to your guests.'

In the living room people were loudly discussing politics, the quality of restaurants, the stalled peace process in the Middle East. I liked their company. All of a sudden the shiva made a lot of sense. The guests were like a big family to me. Something I had never experienced before. They knew perfectly what they needed, in the kitchen and around the house and helped themselves.

Barry was by far the loudest. He had been like that as long as I had known him. Since childhood. He was twelve years older than me.

He had a high position with a well respected weekly magazine, writing about international affairs. His main focus was the Middle East. He was overly loyal to Israel, as long as it didn't concern the Labor Party. His stories were biased, commending Israel, ridiculing Arabs. He was frequently disciplined by his editor-in-chief. Barry called him an anti-Semite. I was convinced that both of them were right.

Barry got away with it, thanks to Elise who was the assistant to the editor-in-chief and had a calming effect on him.

Elise was a petite, quiet woman, born in a German village not far from the Polish border. At age four she lost her parents when inhabitants of her neighborhood were arrested and deported to a labor camp. Her home and the women's clothing factory, owned by her father and two uncles, were confiscated. She remembered it all. The shouting, pushing and hitting soldiers, the flames destroying all of their belongings that had been thrown outside. The soldiers were laughing as they forced her mother to take off her clothes. When she begged them for permission to leave her corset on, they smashed her onto the pavement and raped her, one by one. Elise, her father and brother were forced to watch.

Elise had put a few clothes and a coat hanger of her father's business in a pillowcase which she carried in her little hand. Her other arm carried her favorite doll. Big dogs were barking at her and the others who were arrested. Across the street, she saw how the wife of the butcher got killed by a shot through the head. An amused soldier grabbed Elise's doll, threw it to one of the dogs who immediately shredded it to pieces.

At the street corner Jacov Hirsch, the butcher's son, witnessed what was going on. His mother got killed in front of his eyes. As if paralysed, he held on to his bike.

He belonged to a strongly motivated Zionist youth organization. He tried to persuade his parents to leave the country and go to Palestine. 'We can still do it,' he repeatedly tried to convince his father. 'If we stay they are going to kill us all. Hitler has plans to kill all Jews. There are death camps where people are being gassed in large numbers.'

His mother agreed, but Jacov's father said that he was exaggerating. 'You are young,' he argued. 'You see everything in black and white. When you grow up you will learn that there are nuances. I am not telling you that the Nazis are kosher, but one should never condemn others without giving them the benefit of the doubt. Maybe they will let us stay, maybe if we just do as they say, they will treat us right. Maybe we have to deliver some work in a labor camp. I talked to people who told me that conditions there are not bad at all. There are too many rumors. Why would they first round people up and then put them on a train to a camp to kill them. If that's what they are after, they might as well kill us here and use their trains for military transports. Maybe your mother frightened you, because she has too much time to listen to gossip. I am not going to flee my own country. I am a well respected citizen, I fulfill my duties so why should I listen to a bunch of youngsters, imagining that they can establish their own country?'

The discussions continued. Jacov started his preparations to leave. He obtained falsified travel documents, a passport and a good looking ID. He earned some money at a farm of a non-Jewish family that was supportive.

Now, standing on the street corner, all of his negative predictions got confirmed. It was even worse than he had feared. He saw his parents beaten out of their house, his father's store looted and his mother shot and killed. He couldn't believe his eyes. He had learned of these kinds of roundups and now, now he had nobody left anymore. He stood frozen, while he witnessed his dead mother lying in her own blood; he knew that he would not see his father again. Their house went up in flames. All of his childhood memories, his books, his toys, the ham-radio he had built himself, the stories he wrote about reaching Palestine and working there. His eyes registered what was happening, but his emotions were shut off and would never fully recover. He made eye contact with his father. Neither gave a sign of recognition. He observed Elise's family being thrown out of their house, how a soldier grabbed Elise's doll and threw it at one of the dogs.

He felt an explosion of anger. Jacov stashed his bike and rushed down the street, ignoring several soldiers ordering him to stop. He walked straight up to the car of the officer in charge and started cursing at him. Two soldiers pointed their guns at Jacov.

'What in the name of Der Führer do you think you are doing?' he yelled face to face with the officer. 'You can treat these fucking Jews as pigs, but keep your hands off my little sister. If I tell this to my father, you'll be demoted.'

He turned around, took Elise, put her on his bike and peddled out of the street, yelling and cursing at every soldier.

Together they made a long journey by bicycle and by foot, all the way across Germany, through the Dutch border. It was a long exhausting, nerve wracking trip. They got arrested twice, but Jacov's resistance friends had provided him with state-of-the-art falsified documents and Jacov boasted to the enemy. In Holland he found a foster family for Elise.

A few days later he headed south for Palestine. It became a lengthy, unsuccessful ordeal. He was arrested in France and deported to a death camp in Poland. He jumped off the train in Poland, but could not find a living soul to help him. Someone he approached reported him to the authorities. This time he was put on transport to a labor camp in Germany. He managed to escape by killing two guards with his bare hands.

Aware of the risk, he knocked on the door of a farmhouse. His fear that he would be betrayed again was unsubstantiated this time. He was welcomed with open arms by the German farmer family. Previously they had helped escapees, being glad that they could do something positive in this time of misery.

Jacov had the opportunity to finally rest a few days and was well fed. Through the farmer's resistance connections he obtained new falsified documents and as he left, he had a suitcase with good clean clothes, new shoes and was given a substantial amount of cash.

In 1944 Jacov finally reached the frontline and got in touch with the allied troops in Italy. There he ran into another major disappointment. He witnessed how displaced persons on liberated territory were rounded up at random by American military police. They were taken in trucks to a navy vessel, transporting wounded American soldiers back home. He learned that it was a so-called "rescue mission" ordered by President Roosevelt. During his re-election campaign one of his aides had warned the President that there was a growing number of Americans who were becoming disloyal to him because during his regime, his country had categorically refused to host European refugees seeking shelter.

As a propaganda stunt the President ordered one thousand people to be rescued, Jews and non-Jews. However, to avoid complications, recently liberated people were "rescued," while Hitler had ordered to speed up efforts to dispose of as many Jews as possible and destroy them all. Jacov was crying with anger. The chimneys of the crematoria in Auschwitz and other concentration camps blew the ashes of the gassed into the skies and now, people who miraculously escaped and were displaced where shipped to America? Yes, but unfortunately the President failed to inform the American Immigration Service to let "the rescued" into the country. They were shipped to a concentration camp in Fort Ontario, upstate New York, severely suffering from the cold and isolation. After the war they were set free, but didn't receive any support. Welcome to America! Many of them didn't know if their relatives survived. Cut off from their roots, their remaining family members and what once was home and displaced by the liberator. During the war the British had cut off the escape route to Palestine and this was America's contribution?

'Why don't you bomb Auschwitz?' he reproached an American officer.

'Because the army doesn't make rational decisions,' the friendly man answered.

'We are winning this war because there are so many of us and we were able to switch our economy into a war economy. That's why we are superior. And don't forget that the Russians have done a lot of dirty work for us at the eastern front. Let me give you some friendly advice. If you are looking for rationality and justice, you are in the wrong place at the wrong time. I know all about it.'

The American soldier got Jacov in touch with an officer of a British-Palestinian unit. This man helped him to sign up with a division of the allied forces that later took part in the liberation of Holland.

After the German capitulation he searched for the whereabouts of Elise. He did not know for a fact that she was still alive. After they were reunited it appeared that Elise remembered all of the details of their escape, like a nightmare. Her foster parents had treated her with love and passion and she looked healthy. At age seventeen she married an electronics engineer, a child of a well-to-do sophisticated Catholic family.

Jacov married a British woman he met in the army. They successfully managed a wholesale children's clothing business.

When in the early nineties Germany finally agreed to provide financial compensation for lost properties in the former Republic of

East Germany, Elise asked her friend Jacov, details about her family's business, owned by her deceased father and uncles.

'Do you still have that stupid clothes hanger?' he asked her. 'You hung on to it like other kids do to their blanky. It could have killed us because the name of your father's business was on that hanger and we were traveling with false documents.'

Elise opened a drawer. Underneath a pile of underwear she kept that clothes hanger. Her hands were shaking, she was on the verge of tears.

'Since my arrival in Holland I could not find the courage to look at it,' she told Jacov. 'My husband put it here after we got married.' She stared at it.

"Rosenthal's Fashion Designs" was printed on the hanger, along with an address and phone number.

'Don't get carried away,' Jacov advised her. 'For your own sake, don't file a claim with these bastards. I know them. You'll get stuck with a bunch of unwilling bureaucrats. You won't see a dime and you will only be aggravated and upset in the end.'

Elise disagreed. Her family was robbed. As a matter of principal and justice, that should be compensated.

'I won't get my family back,' she argued. 'But they should pay for their thefts.'

Elise filed a claim via a knowledgeable attorney for the loss of all personal belongings, movables, the clothing factory and looted bank accounts. She received confirmation that the information on the hanger matched the files of the German bureaucrats. She was informed that the factory had been a substantial business with over eighty employees, several trucks, valuable machinery and on a large piece of property. During the war it had been used to produce army uniforms.

Two years later she received an envelope from the German

authorities. She took it to Jacov because she had not spoken any German since age four and was unable to read the documents.

'What they write is that the factory was located on the even-numbered side of the street,' Jacob explained. 'The odd numbers are located in Germany now, the even numbers in Poland. In other words, you are not going to get a dime. Wrong side of the street. I told you so, they always find a way to avoid fulfilling their obligations.' Elise got nothing and once more Jacov's negative way of reasoning was confirmed. "Wrong side of the street."

Elise brought up three children and kept a good job with the editor-in-chief of the foreign affairs magazine. Once a week Barry took her out to lunch. Barry complained about his anti-Semitic editor-in-chief, censoring his articles. Elise tried to help him understand that he could be a little less biased. He never got that message. He loudly maintained that he was right.
I was glad that he became a daily visitor of the shiva.
I could clearly follow his loud monologues over the hurly-burly of the others.
'Nonsense.' I heard him argue. 'Give an Arab one finger and he will take the whole hand. How can you use the phrase "Peace Process" when you are dealing with terrorists and thieves. Perhaps goyim can afford to turn the other cheek each time they get hurt. To us Jews, it has never done any good to wait and see until you get killed.'

Barry lost his parents in 1944, was hidden for a while and then grew up in a strict Catholic orphanage. Whenever I told him that he was a little bit too loud and outspoken, he always used the same phrase.
'You are absolutely right. I am always the loudest, I never shut up and I am opinionated. Oy, in hiding I had to be quiet, in that

Catholic orphanage it was even worse. Now people have to listen to me. Or not, I don't really care. But I can say whatever I want, as loud as I want.'

I could tell by the humorous expression on his face that he had altered the social rules to his liking. Each time he gave his explanation he looked so relieved and happy. That's why we tolerated his noisy lectures in which he went way too far.

On the last day of the shiva he pulled up the driveway flaunting a new car. To make sure that his new purchase did not remain unnoticed, he set off the alarm. This way he managed to manipulate over ten guests to take a peek at his new toy, defying the freezing cold.

Had I been a business person with a future vision I would have been a wealthy person by now. At age seven I invented the first alarm system. In fact it was an "early warning system" for my mother approaching my bedroom, either to hit me during an attack of hysteria or hug me and take me with her into her bed. My attempt to protect myself was a result of her unpredictable mood swings. Staying awake was impossible. The shelter underneath my bed also provided insufficient protection to modern warfare. She had invented her own nerve gas, a bucket of bleach that she threw at me while I was hiding underneath the bed. Gasping and vomiting I crawled away. She took me by the legs and smashed me against the wall as if she was cleaning a carpet.

The moment I apparently was "dust free" her mood drastically changed.

'You are my most precious treasure on earth,' she whispered in my ear while I was struggling to escape her hug that pushed me onto her huge, nude breasts.

That endearment didn't provide any prospect that the violence wouldn't return all of a sudden. Or that she wouldn't terrorize people by phone, calling them at random, even in the middle of the night.

'I gave birth to a little devil,' she would say. 'That child is mean. I will have him locked up.'

Before he left for Germany, I had performed a secret transaction with my neighbor friend Ludo. In the middle of the night I had exchanged some candies and a toy car for a battery, a small electric bell, some wires and a switch. During my mother's absence I put the switch underneath the carpet in the hall, ran a wire to my bed, put the battery underneath my mattress and the little buzzer underneath my bed.

After I hid the wires I immediately tested my new high tech invention. I stepped on the carpet and it worked! The buzzer went off. Now I had an "early warning system" so I would no longer be surprised while asleep. I couldn't wait to test my newly installed defense system in a real situation. I did not have to wait too long.

That night my mother exploded over a hole in my pants. What would follow was predictable.

'I am making him walk around in shorts,' I heard her yell from the living room. 'If he falls he will have a hole in his knee and not in his pants. Knees heal for free and it will make him get used to the cold in winter. That may be a good lesson, but first I am going to teach him a lesson now.'

I heard her heavy footsteps approach my bedroom door. As she stepped on the carpet, the buzzer went off. It worked! With a victorious feeling I dived underneath my bed and pulled a pillow over my head, waiting for her to storm into my room, but the door remained closed. There were a few seconds of silence followed by a big bang and the sound of breaking glass. The switch underneath the carpet had created a little bump. Due to her tremendous weight she tripped over it, fell forward and ploughed into a mirror at the end of the hallway.

I carefully peeked around the door. She sat on the floor, surrounded by shards, but did not have a scratch. She was yelling at the top of her lungs. I did not wait for her to get up. I ran out of the back door into the garden in my pajamas and climbed on top of the shed where we kept coal for the heater.

From this safe position I quietly watched her yelling in the garden.

'As far as I'm concerned you may freeze to death, you dirty rat. Finally an easy way to get rid of you.'

The coast was clear now. She closed the back door with a big bang and locked it. As I tried to get up I fell through the roof of the shed and landed in the black coal.

It became a long cold winter night in the dark dust. However, every time I memorized the picture of my mother on the floor, surrounded by the fragments of the mirror, I smiled.

The next morning I waited until the housekeeper arrived. Her presence would reduce the chance of being beaten up.

To my big surprise my mother started laughing as I came in, black from the coal dust and shivering from the cold.

'That's what happens when you are a mischief,' she smiled. 'Don't you think that you have invented it. My brother and I also did these kinds of things. My father, God rest his soul, always had to laugh about us. Let me prepare you a nice warm bath.'

Her cheerfulness was frightening. Being beaten-up hurts, mood changes from intense hugs and happiness into sudden anger, violence, mostly without any reason, was torture. At a young age I was totally brainwashed. Also because my father acted as if all was normal.

A year later the physical violence came to a sudden stop after she approached me to beat me up and - without realizing what I was doing - I punched her hard in the face. After a few seconds of silence she started to laugh. The physical violence ended there, once and forever.

I couldn't understand why right after my test program of the alarm system, my mother was not angry and gently scrubbed off the coal dust with a brush and soap. I was disgusted by soap and lighter fluid. The fear for lighter fluid was realistic. My mother once cleaned my ears with it, causing burns and leaving me almost deaf for weeks.
Soap nauseated me.
The teacher once asked my class, 'who knows how we make soap?'
I did.
'Go ahead,' the teacher said.
'They make soap from dead people,' I answered.
The entire class started laughing.
'Who taught you this wisdom, or did you make it up yourself?'
'My mother told me that she knows somebody who made soap out of dead people.'
'And where do we find this unique factory, egg head? Or did you make it up?'
'No,' I protested. 'In a concentration camp.'
The class started laughing again, much louder now because my classmates realized that there was an eminent conflict in the air.
'Can you tell the class what a concentration camp is?' the teacher proceeded.
'I don't really know,' I admitted. 'There are barracks stuffed with people who are being gassed and burnt. The soap is made from the ashes.'
'Nonsense,' the teacher said. 'There are no longer concentration camps. You must learn to answer my questions in a proper manner.

You are living in a fantasy world. Well, they don't give good grades there.'

'But they burned my grandfather and grandmother there,' I protested again. 'I didn't make it up at all. They also burned my uncles and aunts and made soap out of them.'

The teacher now became angry.

'You go see the principal. He will deal with you.'

The principal gave me a letter for my parents so I would be punished for my misbehavior. That happened.

A few weeks later I asked my mother if they really made soap out of people. She confirmed this.

Until today this story comes to mind, washing my hands or showering.

My alarm turned into a fiasco. But, maybe had I pursued, I would have owned the patent of the sophisticated system in Barry's new car.

The shiva was almost over. I still felt numb, almost paralyzed. I just let people be, at home and in the office. Business went on as usual, also without Daisy.

Hanukah and New Year's Eve passed by. I politely turned down invitations from friends and neighbors.

My beloved ones fortunately quit asking how I was doing. In all honesty I couldn't objectively answer that question. It felt too confusing. How are you? Compared to what? To last year, a week ago, yesterday, to the time that Daisy was alive?

I was healthy, could look back on an excellent marriage, had dear and loyal friends and was young enough to face new challenges. But that was not the way it felt. I became more and more lost and was unable to concentrate. After attentively reading a newspaper I had no clue as to what I had just read. I panicked in a supermarket because of the profusion of items. Actually, I preferred not leaving my house. A couple of times I dressed up for an early meeting. I fixed breakfast, brewed coffee, before discovering that it was three o'clock in the morning. Sleeping became impossible. Sometimes I dozed off for a little while on the sofa. I couldn't lie on the bed that I had shared with Daisy for so long. There were still a few of her hairs on her pillow, her delicious smell was still around. The bedroom had become a haunted area. I had to leave my house, there were too many memories attached to it, but it would take months before I had the courage to do so.

6

I was looking for a destination where I felt comfortable, protected and that was familiar to me. The first step outside was a far but safe one. I flew to San Francisco, booked a room at the Mark Hopkins Hotel were Daisy and I had met the first time.

Way back, after a business conversation at the restaurant The Top of The Mark, overlooking San Francisco, my host Dick took me down to the lobby. His wife Beverly was waiting for us, sitting at a table near the grand piano with another woman. She introduced me to her old high school roommate, Daisy. We chatted and enjoyed the beautiful classical music that was performed in the luxurious ambiance. We stayed until after midnight. Our pleasure came to an abrupt end when the pianist started to play the American anthem. Everyone in the lobby stood up, put their hands on their hearts and sung out loud.

'Sometimes I think that we copied a lot from the Germans in our country,' Dick said. 'Let's bail this joint.'

Beverly invited me for a nightcap at their pretty penthouse, not far from the hotel.

On our way Daisy and I exchanged a few words. She told me she was living in La Jolla, near San Diego. On the roof terrace of Dick and Beverly's home it became obvious to me that meeting Daisy had been pre-arranged. After about ten minutes Beverly and Dick retired, leaving Daisy and me with an excellent bottle of wine. I found it a nice gesture. As a real Yiddishe mama, Beverly never gave up acting as a semi-personal matchmaker. I was not really comfortable with this situation. I was old enough to establish my own contacts. An affair with Beverly's old friend could ruin my long lasting friendship with Dick and her, if it didn't work out too well. Besides, I did not feel ready for a long-term relationship.

Earlier that day, my brother Eric, had warned me of the dangers of matrimony, after he explained at length about the dark clouds overshadowing his marriage.

'In Hebrew we call a wedding a Hatuna. That's a good expression, because like a tuna fish you are de-boned and canned,' he joked.

'That's precisely my greatest fear,' I replied, joining his act. Women are like mice. They silently sneak into your life. Dating means wasting your money on lousy food at expensive noisy restaurants, but you may have a good time. Later she comes to your house to spend the night. You may have a great time. If so, she will visit more frequently. You may have a wonderful time.

Suddenly you'll find some nylons, sexy slips and bras in one of your drawers. This is when all alarm bells should be activated. But, we men don't think rationally. We ignore the first concrete evidence that she is moving in. Naive as you are you step into quicksand. Suitcases, boxes, plastic bags are being moved into your house. She puts her outfits into your closets. Your clothes are being moved into plastic camping closets where you don't want them and can't find them. Your house is being rearranged. So snugly, that female touch you have always missed. Knickknacks throughout your house and her teddy bear on "her" pillow on "her side" of the bed. Only now you admit to yourself that it's too late to correct your miscalculation. During the last critical phase she starts changing systems that have worked well for you throughout your life. Furniture is being moved, paintings, your mail opened, bank statements checked. As an excuse to go through your pockets, she neatly puts your clothes on hangers. Based on what she finds, you are being questioned mildly, severely or tortured with the silent treatment.'

'You are completely right,' Eric responded. 'But you always have pulled the emergency brake in time, so you don't yet know what's next. I do. She'll determine if you are going on a vacation and if so, when and where to. She'll decide which car you are going to buy and what is good or bad for you. Bye, bye freedom. No matter what you do, working, dining, drinking, smoking, you are always accused of doing too much or too little. If something goes wrong, she tells you, *"you should have...."* Each time you get lost in a strange city or when it rains in Paris, *you* are being blamed.

We is only being used in positive cases. "*We*" have negotiated a good mortgage. However, when the interest rates go down a week later, or Wall Street collapses, she'll tell you that *"you"* should have checked it out better. "If *you* would have...." Take a look at contact ads. "Charming lady, good sense of humor is looking for a financially secure…." Right. Translation: "I am almost over the hill, want a wealthy schlemiel and just wait until I forget my sense of humor and show my real self." I have had it. Irene interferes with phone conversations or listens in to them. "To whom did you talk? What did they say?" All women are Gestapo's, especially my own wife.'

'I sure hope that she isn't listening in to this conversation,' I said.

'Are you out of your mind? I am not suicidal. I call from my office. However, I hope she is not sneaking into my e-mail right now.'

'Dad warned us when we were small,' I added. 'He used to say that the woman is the policeperson of the house. She is the one to implement rules and regulations. Disobey her and you are a dead man. The bitch knows what's best for her husband. She is the one who orders his food in a restaurant. "No waiter, this steak filet is too chewy for my husband. You see, he has a weak stomach." He cannot even get dressed by himself. He automatically puts on whatever she puts out for him. If she doesn't put a pair of shoes on the right spot, he walks out of the house wearing socks. He doesn't know how to fry an egg. Every time she leaves him alone for a few days, she prepares his meals prior to her departure and puts them in plastic containers in the freezer, with precise instructions on when to eat what and how long to put it in the microwave. If he would consume his Monday ration on Sunday the whole system would collapse. If she dies first, he will walk around nude and starve to death.'

'Why am I such a sissy?' Eric asked. 'There is a new carpet in the living room. Or should I say, *we* have new carpet. Now, when I come home from work she tells me to take off my shoes, and I do it. In my own house. All women are Gestapo's. Take my advice, keep screwing around and don't get involved too much. But you too, my dear brother, will follow your penis one day. All men do so, only to be suppressed by a Gestapo the rest of their lives.'

'Why are you smiling?' Daisy asked. 'Funny thoughts?'
I stared at the beautiful view of the lights of San Francisco by night. 'Maybe I'll tell you someday,' I answered.
I tried to figure out a discreet way to leave. It was one o 'clock in the morning. I was getting cold and shivered for a second.

Daisy put her arm around my neck, pushed my head against her shoulder and covered me with her mink jacket. A warm, overwhelming sensation went through my body. A sensation I had never experienced before. Somehow this was the most comfortable and safest place I had ever been.

My mothers' hugs had been disgusting. My father had never touched nor kissed me. I had been avoiding hugs. Now this was a new godly experience. For the first time in my life I felt nurtured, relaxed and without a worry in the world. My closed eyes were filled with beautiful colors.

I felt her heart beat, sensed the smell of her hair, skin and breath. In that wonderful cloud of happiness she took me by the hand to my hotel.

The next morning we took a bath together. Her messy makeup accentuated a lack of sleep. We both had to leave for an appointment, but first she had to change at Dick's and Beverly's. She looked in the mirror wearing her black evening dress from the night before.

'I look like a hooker,' she said.

She asked the taxi driver if business had been good during the night.

'No complaints,' he answered. 'How about yours?'

Luckily my work required me to stay in Los Angeles for a while. I booked a bungalow in the beautiful garden of the former Ambassador Hotel. An oasis of silence, a paradise of flowers in a big city. The hotel no longer exists, but the memories do. Daisy moved in with me. We made trips to Mexico, took a chopper to Catalina Island, enjoying the scenery, rented a small boat, surrounded by dolphins and seals. She seduced me into many afternoon naps. She fell in love and I learned how to love her. We were in heaven. The only dissonant took place at the residence of the Dutch Consul-General. Daisy felt like I spent too much attention flirting with a good looking woman.

She became irritated and threatened that she would leave the party alone.

I just said, 'Okay, if that's what you want.'

She was aggravated and walked out. Half an hour later I went to the men's room. As I walked in Daisy switched the lights on and locked the door from the inside. She undressed me and we made passionate love, leaning on the sink. Only later we discovered that the window was open, making it very likely that the guests in the garden and the swimming pool must have enjoyed the entire happening.

Shortly afterward she moved in with me in my house in Ridgefield, Connecticut. We never had any misunderstandings, we remained in love and our love grew. We became inseparable. The beginning of ultimate happiness that was a new, godly experience to me.

That's why I had decided to return to the place where we first met. A round of honor for her and myself.

7

On the flight to San Francisco I wondered if I was escaping Daisy's death or if I was on my way to a new future. Rationally I knew that I had to carry on towards a new future, but there were no matching emotions. Maybe it was too early to think about it. After a loss of a beloved one you are lost and emotionally numb for a while.

My thoughts were interrupted by the captain who told us that we had reached our cruising altitude of thirty-four thousand feet and that the outside temperature was freezing cold; it made my day. With a fatherly voice he informed the passengers that he had switched off the fasten seat belt sign. Why do you need a captain to pull that switch off? Any schlemiel can do that. We also were 'a little ahead of schedule.'

'Just like the Titanic,' I thought.

A friendly smiling flight attendant served food that looked and smelled as if it had been eaten before. I ordered a scotch instead and almost dozed off. I tried to figure out how traumatic a loss could be. My friend Molly lost a son. Her life will never be the same. She was unable to compare life before and after it happened. After such a disaster your brain should be recalibrated, but an instrument to do so has yet to be invented. My parents lost their entire family; Elise lost everything except for a hanger and still carried on. According to my Dutch friends Ilse and Alex, I was unable to feel what the loss of a family member meant.

They had claimed the exclusive rights of these emotions. Monopolized them.

'We returned from hell,' Alex said. 'We lost everyone and faced burning corpses in Auschwitz. These images are forever embedded in our minds. You will find another woman one day.'

Alex was forced to carry the deceased to the crematorium. Some of them he recognized, including his father.

'Every day we saw that smoke, ashes of people being blown away. It is a miracle that I was not amongst them. Coincidence. I was selected for the gas chamber. I lost my strength due to starvation. I was convinced that I was going to be killed. At the last moment one of these bastard SS officers approached me and said: 'Hey you, you are going to live, because I am in a good mood. It's my birthday.' He gave me some clothes and I walked back along the long queue of those who were condemned. I avoided their eyes. Later that day he forced me on the ground. I had to kiss his boots to show my appreciation for him to let me live. He took his rifle, pointed it at my head and told me that he was going to kill me after all. He unlocked his weapon, put his finger on the trigger, cursed me. Then he told me that he had changed his mind again because "he had given me his word as an officer." He beat me unconscious and left me bleeding in the dirt. I lost most of my teeth, my back was injured and my nose was broken. Since then I haven't experienced a moment without pain, but somehow I'm still grateful to that man for saving my life. He could have killed me, but he didn't. That was suffering that you will never understand. The fear, the pain, the hunger, the loneliness, the cold. The isolation, trying to survive a fenced hell in a world that didn't seem to care. They didn't care. After the war, when I returned to Amsterdam, people were hostile. Someone told me that he regretted that I survived, because there was a housing shortage.

I ran into a goy who had been working for my father. He took me home. Prior to his deportation, my father gave him all of his savings. It was a substantial amount. He had kept it, hoping that some of the family would survive. I thanked God because I was penniless. All I had were the clothes I was wearing. My father's former employee advised me to take the money to the National Netherlands Bank. During the occupation, the Nazis decided to change bank notes. Everyone could go to any bank to change the old notes for new ones. Except the Jews. It had been too risky to change my father's savings, because the amount did not match with his tax returns. The President of the Netherlands Bank, Dutchman, Rost van Tonningen, was a feared Nazi.

After the liberation, the clerk at the Netherlands Bank took my money and told me that it was too late for me to change it into valid currency. I desperately went to the highest manager, who told me that it was none of his concern that I had been in Auschwitz when the new bank notes were issued. 'It could be black money,' he said. I did not receive a dime.

Shortly afterward I received an income tax invoice for my father for the years 1943, 1944 and 1945. I explained that my father died in Auschwitz in August 1943. They couldn't care less. I was forced to pay. After that, I got a steep bill from Amsterdam University because I had not notified them that I would be absent. Can you believe it? I was arrested and deported to Auschwitz. I told them that I sent them a certified letter which they must have received, because the Auschwitz Postal Service was extremely accurate and service minded. They didn't get it. I had to pay the full sum. I blame the Royal family for fleeing to London when Holland was occupied. There was a so-called government in exile in London, but in fact the

Nazis got the whole bureaucratic infrastructure as a present. Civil servants, police and the military police. So the Germans had an easy task. Dutch police arrested most of the Jews and made sure that they were deported by Dutch trains. That's why only ten percent survived. Years later we discovered that banks had stolen money from accounts from deported Jews and insurance companies had destroyed their policies. The Jews were plundered. Even our household goods and furniture were professionally stolen. You are lucky that you were born after the war, God bless you.'

In some respects Alex was right. Even though I had heard his monologue almost each time we met, I was unable to see what he saw, I had not experienced the terror, hunger or cold. The loneliness I did understand. The fear and pain were different. I was anguished by the SchutzStaffel (SS) whom I had never seen. He had been brutally faced with them.

Alex and his wife felt that the post-war generation could not fully understand them. That's why they tried harder each time to explain it, especially to their own children. One of them was hospitalized in a mental institution for years.

I would have done anything to show my understanding, but there was a gap in our communication. Therefore it was impossible to share my grief with them after Daisy died. They brought me homemade cookies and chopped liver instead.

When I arrived at the Mark Hopkins Hotel in San Francisco, I discovered that little had changed. Only the piano player had been replaced by a pianola, a funny doll sitting on the music-stool in a tuxedo, to cover up that the piano was playing on automatic pilot. In the lobby, where Daisy and I had met, people were enjoying high tea.

I had my luggage delivered to my room and took the elevator to The Top of The Mark to have a drink and watch the sunset over the city. From my table I saw the roof terrace of the penthouse were Dick and Beverly used to live. I couldn't go all the way back to the "scene of the crime" because they had recently moved. I stared at the roof terrace where Daisy had put me under her jacket and into her heart. I had arrived in the city alone, back then, and now returned alone again. I felt tears running down my cheeks. A couple at another table stared at me. I left money for my drink and rushed to my room. A flood of memories streamed through my head, dripping outside through tears from my eyes. I lay down on the bed with a cold, wet towel on my face until dinnertime.

An old friend, Dave and his wife Leslie, had invited me to a nearby restaurant. I had known Dave since childhood. He grew up in a house with parents who were always arguing. It was the only way for them to communicate. The atmosphere at his home is engraved in my memory.

When his dad was hungry he did not ask for food but blamed his wife. 'Now I have another migraine attack because you never serve a meal on time. Do you only think about yourself?'

When he found a fishbone in his flounder he dramatically acted, 'I could have choked to death.'

Every day he lost his keys. We heard him complain. 'Now where did you put my keys? I can never find anything in my own house.'

His wife yelled back.

'Is there anything I can do right in this house. I cook for you, do your laundry, clean up after you, I am being treated like a slave.'

The argument continued in Yiddish or Polish, so we had a hard time understanding.

Dave's dad had an Auschwitz number tattooed on his arm. He never talked about it. Instead he talked to himself in Polish.

He often locked himself in the bathroom. He just sat there for lengthy periods of time, in the dark. Sometimes we could hear him cry. We didn't ask why.

Only once we tried. He stared at us for a while and said: 'You kids wouldn't understand, you just wouldn't.' Then he kissed us on the cheek.

'You can't trust anyone in this world,' he warned us. 'No one. Think for yourself. Others don't do that for you. If I had counted on others I wouldn't be here today.'

His abhorrence for uniforms lead to confrontations. Once he ran into a temporary detour. A friendly police officer provided him with an alternative route. Dave's father ignored the advice and got stuck for hours due to a big union demonstration. However, he was proud that he had followed his own will.

'I don't take instructions from a teenager in uniform. We live in a free nation, I can go wherever I want to, whenever I want to.'

He refused to pay parking tickets, his car got towed away because it was either blocking a police car or parked in a loading zone.

'I put my car where I want to,' he proudly announced, as if it was a victory to outsmart the system. Police knew him and usually let him off the hook.

It was a house full of anxiety, transmitted to Dave who meanwhile had anxieties passed them on to his wife, but especially to his two sons. Anxiety, fear and nervousness together formed a package of fast, transmittable disease. A violent, deadly virus.

Dave had copied part of his father's behavior, especially trying to outsmart others. But he also liked the challenge of risky and dangerous situations, balancing on the edge. During the early years of his marriage he had all sorts of affairs. He was a womanizer. He loved the anxiety and fear of his wife finding out, which of course she did after a while.

'How come I always have guilty feelings?' he asked me.

'Maybe you are guilty,' I answered. 'You keep creating unnecessary situations that scare you, because other people make you feel guilty. In fact it proves that you have a conscience.'

'That's not what it is,' he responded. 'Everyone, my parents, Leslie, they all constantly give me the guilt-trip.'

There came an abrupt end to his sexual escapades after one of his girlfriends became pregnant. Dave got sued and Leslie threatened to leave him. His friends did not show much sympathy, so he was forced into monogamy. He found alternatives to satisfy his need to dangerously challenge the system. He got involved with businesses that were impenetrable to outsiders. Enormous financial transactions took place, but nobody knew what for. He went through numerous bankruptcies but maintained the lifestyle of a wealthy gentleman. Leslie objected to Dave travelling first class on short flights.

'I get claustrophobic sitting in too small a seat surrounded by three hundred goyim and their crying children. I need space,' he told her.

He never spent the night in a normal hotel room, but only in the most luxurious suites available.

'When I am on a business trip I need to feel comfortable,' he explained. 'I can't work sitting on a bed. I need a desk and an office.'

His two sons had copied his lifestyle with his permission. One studied arts for several years, the other studied law at an expensive university that was not very demanding. They drove around in costly automobiles, chit-chatting on their cell phones and took costly trips, all on Dave's expenses.

Dave's spending pattern was obvious, but where his sources of income came from nobody really knew. Once I made an unsuccessful attempt to get an idea of the nature of his business. He proudly showed me a complicated business plan on a futuristic alternative power plant, to be built in northern Canada. The plant would produce energy at low cost without expelling pollutants or dangerous waste.

'It's a technological, environmental miracle, the end of global warming,' he explained. He proudly showed me the cover of the glossy presentation carrying the tentative title: "Eco-energy, A Safe Way Into The Future," and a state-of-the-art drawing of a futuristic building in the snow, surrounded by forest with deer and happy looking grizzly bears.

He explained to me that the financing had almost been settled.

'I won't open the bottle of champagne yet, but it's waiting in the refrigerator to be opened any day now, so keep your fingers crossed.'

'When do you estimate the deal to be finalized?' I asked.

'With a little luck in a few weeks. More like a matter of two weeks than a matter of months.'

This conversation took place two decades ago. Still the project is alive, although the title on the cover of his business plan has changed several times, as well as the anticipated location and additional budgets and investors.

Dave always stood by his friends to whom he was extremely loyal. A charming, humorous, endearing but weird man. If he had put all of his talents in real business, he would have made it big. An extremely intelligent person, analytical, straight to the point in five languages he spoke fluently and without a trace of an accent. In his deluxe office, at a prime location of the city, overlooking the Bay Bridge he spent his days making lengthy long distance calls and smoking big cigars behind his antique desk. He was addicted to telephones. Dave used to call his friends from all over the world. From limousines, airplanes, one of his suites, just to touch base. After Daisy died he called every day, sometimes twice, from Canada, a Hong Kong restaurant, the most expensive hotel in Paris, a New York theater. Always with a proper, loyal attitude, carefully listening and never failing to end the conversation with a humorous story. His bankruptcies did not seem to bother him too much. With a lot of devotion he continued working tirelessly on his project. With a new company, letterhead and always new investors. He beat every system to maintain his lifestyle of the rich and famous.

'If you want to be successful, you must try to pick the flowers over the edges of the steepest gullies,' was his slogan.

'Oh yes,' his wife Leslie once responded. 'Reach too far and you will get smashed to death in the canyon below.'

'Not necessarily, darling. Business involves taking calculated risks.'

Leslie gave up.

As usual Dave's culinary choice was excellent, the wines superb, the conversation entertaining and charming. Of course Dave had to make several intercontinental phone calls from the latest model cellular phone and send some emails. At my request the waiter made some snapshots with a Polaroid camera. Leslie and I enjoying the meal, side by side, Dave on his phone, smoking a big cigar.

'Good news,' he explained after the third call. 'Knock on wood, but I'm sure that I can finalize the entire deal before the end of the month now. I am not going to celebrate before the ink of the signatures on the contract has dried, but all pieces of the puzzle are together now. Tomorrow I am off to Tokyo and that's it.'

'How many times have I heard that?' asked Leslie who did not expect an answer.

After dinner I wanted to walk the few blocks back to the hotel, but Dave insisted on driving me there in his chauffeured limousine that had been parked in front of the restaurant. On the way he poured fine *cognac* and lit another big cigar. Arriving at the hotel I offered them a night cap. As usual Dave did not allow me to pay.

'With compliments and the warmest regards of mister Mahisoto,' he toasted, introducing yet another name to his long list of investors.

Leslie gave me a picture that a waiter took a few years earlier at a Japanese grill. Leslie making jokes to Daisy, me laughing at Dave making long distance calls from his cellular phone. I put the photograph in the envelope, together with the picture that the waiter had just taken at the restaurant.

'There used to be four of us,' said Dave. 'Now we are one down, three more to go. Who is going to be next?'

'Do we have permission to first finish our drinks before we jump into our coffins?' Leslie asked.

'I did not encourage anyone to hurry,' Dave said. 'It's just reality. One day there will be a picture with just two of us.'

'Or four,' Leslie responded. 'No one is irreplaceable.'

The bartender started to clean up and we kissed goodbye. Dave and Leslie drove off in their limousine, I went back to my room.

I put the two restaurant pictures on the dresser and stoically glanced at them.

'No one is irreplaceable,' I repeated Leslie's words.

Staring at Daisy in the picture, I felt emotionally paralyzed. I was functional, rational, but my feelings were dead or numb.

Thoughts flashed through my head, as if they were fired by a machine gun. An uncontrollable explosion of sad memories that all used to be happy.

My visit to San Francisco had not created an emotional awakening, but dining and talking to Dave and Leslie had been pleasant. One good, new memory for later.

I was running my office remotely by phone, fax and e-mail. Everything went well without me. I totally lost interest and gave Ron and Meta more of a mandate to operate without my supervision. I couldn't care less. My interest had vanished completely.

I spent several weeks with an old acquaintance of Daisy's, helping her to set up a business after she divorced. We worked long hours.

At a restaurant I wondered why people were staring at us. It was my dinner companion who attracted the attention. She was stunningly beautiful, her face radiated intelligence, love and compassion. I realized she had been flirting with me for weeks. Had I spent two weeks with her and not noticed her appearance? Had I lost it completely now? My appetite, the need for sleep, my involvement with my office? Had I been totally insensible to an endearing beauty who had tried her utmost to please me and get my personal attention?

A month after Daisy's accident a friend in the Netherlands invited me to stay with him for a weekend at his gorgeous farmhouse. As I woke up, I noticed that it had been snowing. The farmland was white, there were sheep on the dike and winter trees with snow-covered branches in the early morning light. Prettier than a painting by one of the old Dutch masters. My eyes registered it, my brain told me that it was beautiful but it did not generate any emotion. Feelings seemed to have died, even during frequent crying fits.

8

I used my stay at the American west coast to visit some acquaintances in Los Angeles. Before Daisy and I moved to Holland we had lived several years in Brentwood, not far from the former O.J. Simpson Estate. Sometimes we saw him at the Brentwood Mart, with his children. Little did we know that he would become a criminal television celebrity.

As a matter of courtesy I paid a short visit to Daisy's sister Tina and her husband Carl in Manhattan Beach. We had never really socialized. She and Daisy were not the best of friends and there was the issue of the geographical distance between Manhattan Beach and Connecticut, later Soesterberg, Holland.
Tina was the prototype of a "laid back" Californian. She and her husband were not interested in anything out of state, let alone Europe, which was considered to be another planet with different kinds of people that speak strange languages.
As a European they treated me as a "foreign alien" who made transatlantic phone calls in strange languages, read foreign newspapers and literature. As for me, I was not interested in their small talk about cars, the weather, money, golf and sales in shopping malls.
Carl was a stockbroker, so he had to get up at three in the morning

in order to be at work before the opening bell on Wall Street. When he returned at three o 'clock in the afternoon, he took a can of beer, put his sneakers - which he never took off - on the coffee table and watched a sports channel on television.

'How is business going?' he asked me.

'They consult me when necessary, but I am not really involved at the moment,' I answered. 'I have other things on my mind now.'

'Are you still whining about Daisy?' Tina asked. 'She is dead and you can't make her come back. Grow up, take charge of your life, you are emotionally dependent. Exactly like the shrink on talk radio described. Why don't you attend one of these self-esteem weekends?'

'We were interdependent,' I responded. 'That happens when two nice people share their lives, you know?'

'When are you going back home?' Carl asked, probably to avoid a further escalation of our discussion.

'I don't yet know where home is,' I answered. 'Perhaps I won't return to the house where we lived. I'm still making my mind up.'

'You don't even know where you live and you neglect your business?' Tina asked, agitated.

'Maybe I'll let Ron buy me out,' I said. 'To set myself free.'

'But what are you going to do for a living?'

'Make sure that I am not dying. It was fun running the office together with Daisy, but now it is contaminated.'

'You're crazy,' Tina argued. 'You and Daisy put all your energy in it for years, got it off the ground, made it successful and profitable and now you call it quits and let Ron have it all?'

'First of all, I'm not crazy,' I deliberately provoked her. 'I asked myself that question many times and realized that I would never have asked myself that question, had I been crazy. On the other issues you are completely right. I have a great future behind me. I have been a workaholic my entire life. Always shoved my aches and pains under the carpet by working around the clock. If I go on like that, I'll become an overweight, frustrated, brain dead old man without a love life, hanging on the sofa, drinking beer, watching baseball on television, wasting my life away.'

My timing was perfect. Carl had just returned from the kitchen with a six pack of beer, switched the television on and put his feet on the coffee table. I wanted to get out of there.

During earlier conversations, like her husband, Tina had tried to find out if Daisy left a will, and if so, if she could count on a financial surprise. She was about to bring up this issue again.

'If you are thinking about making a posthumous profit from your deceased sister, forget it,' I said.

'We need to talk about it,' Tina persisted.

'You do. I don't,' I answered determinedly. 'Ed McMahon died, so did your sister. It's been a privilege meeting with you in person again. I wish you both happiness and wisdom. I didn't come here to argue but to say goodbye in a respectful manner. As far as I am concerned, my mission is accomplished.'

I never heard from her or Carl again which I did not regret.

9

Contradictory to the cold shower I received from Daisy's sister, an exuberant reception was waiting for me at Café Montmartre; a small French bistro in Santa Monica that Daisy and I frequently visited, even when we lived in Connecticut. We became close friends with Pierre, the owner. He had always been upbeat and caring, although he had little reason to be happy. His domestic situation was sorrowful.

Pierre married a Belgian woman, Simone, who had moved to the United States in 1957, at age eighteen.

Prior to her parents' deportation to Auschwitz where they were murdered, they had found a safe place for Simone with a Catholic family that was willing to adopt her. Her first memories where of her parents abandoning her forever at age three. She was unable to "forgive" them. To the outside world, she had made it through the war without major incidents. She went to school, was well fed and appeared well taken care of. However her foster parents disgusted her. They were strict and controlling and would not let her leave the house until she was eighteen. She had accumulated some savings and right after her eighteenth birthday she bought herself a one-way ticket to Boston, where she had a remote relative who helped her to get a job and a small apartment.

Men her age loved her. She was a pretty young woman with beautiful blue eyes and deep dark hair. She never showed any interest until she met Pierre.

He was born and raised in Algeria, but the political and social situation forced him to move. Like many North African Jews he tried to build a new life in Paris but decided to leave, because North Africans were being discriminated against. They called them "pieds noires," indicating that they were filthy people with dirty feet.

'First they baited me out of Algeria because I was a Jew, then the French provoked me for my North African heritage,' he once said.

He too moved to the United States, studied Business Administration and supported himself. Just after his studies he met Simone. After they got married they moved to Los Angeles where he opened a restaurant that earned the outstanding reputation of being a truly haute cuisine venue and for Pierre's personable, cordial service.

Pierre and Simone spoiled their three children rotten, literately giving them everything they asked or whined for, which was a lot. But they did not receive the parental attention they really needed. Thus they became impossible southern Californian beach creatures who drove their German convertibles from mall to mall.

The atmosphere at home rapidly became disastrous. A few years after their chupah it became clear that Simone had been sexually abused by her stepfather during her years in hiding. All these years her stepfather had threatened her that he would reveal her real identity to the authorities if she talked about it.

'They will bring you to Auschwitz, you'll be gassed and burned, just like your parents,' he threatened her.

After she had told Pierre - hardly voluntarily - she refused to talk about her past ever again. His suggestion to seek professional help infuriated her.

'Are you telling me that I am insane?'

Endless discussions followed, each without any result.

Simone hid the rest of her life in deep depression and could only keep herself going by severe obsessive compulsion. She lived in a beautiful villa. Pierre gave her money to decorate it, but instead she rented some ugly, cheap furniture. She imposed rules and regulations for mostly everything in the house. So many, that she never got a thing done.

It took her two days to finish one load of laundry. She invented a whole new ritual. First she put laundry in the washing machine, poured in half a bucket of water and let that soak for an hour. She would sit and wait next to her washing machine. After exactly sixty minutes she added detergent, half an hour later, some more.

When her children laughed at her, telling her that she was washing by hand in an automatic washing machine, she became indignant.

'I am not going to ruin our good clothes,' was her response. 'This way you really get them clean. If I just dump it in that machine and turn it on, I will trash them after a few months.'

Every night there was an argument about dinner. Half an hour prior to dinnertime, Simone went into the children's rooms to tell them to go freshen up and dress appropriately. When they finally sat down at the dinner table there was no food. Every day Simone forgot to go grocery shopping.

Her refrigerator was almost empty. There was a cupboard with hundreds of little jars of homemade jams and marmalades that nobody ever touched.

Each time, she made the commitment to her children to go grocery shopping the next day, but it never happened. If the children wanted to prepare something themselves she sabotaged them by interfering. Each kitchen utensil the kids wanted to use, she put back in a drawer the moment they didn't pay attention. Every bowl to be used to whip some eggs or fix a salad was grabbed away, was thoroughly cleaned and wiped dry before she put it in the dishwasher. Each time the children turned around, something was missing. Often they told her to leave the kitchen, which she did. Only to return a couple of minutes later, with a big smile, to continue her irritating moves.

When the children put whatever they had used in the dishwasher she took it out, washed and dried everything before she put it back in the dishwasher.

'That's the way to keep things orderly and clean in the house,' she informed her children who paid little attention to her.

Pierre never saw the first half of a movie. Every time he wanted to take her out to the theater, she loitered, completing her checklist. She put all items exactly on the spot where they belonged, folded newspapers and put them away, went through the whole house to check if lights were switched off in rooms that were unused and provided the children with lengthy warnings about possible disasters during her absence. Pierre used to get upset because she refused to speed it up. However he discovered that his remarks were counterproductive, for she would then explain to him in detail why the house could burn down if you didn't unplug the toaster or an iron. Once in the car she insisted to go back into the house to double check all electrical outlets and make sure that the coffee maker was switched off. Unconsciously she had the desire to burn the house down. By the time they arrived at the movie theater, they were just in time for the intermission.

Arguments accumulated, mainly because the children and Pierre refused to live by all the rules that Simone had created. Even though she had no clue as to what her children were learning in school, she insisted to get involved with their homework, irritating them with lengthy stories about her childhood at school. She checked and interfered with everything they were doing, never leaving them a moment of privacy. When they were off to school she entered their rooms and "reorganized" their desks. The oldest one put a lock on her door at age twelve. The next day Simone had it removed by a locksmith. She was a master in creating a problem for each solution.

Every day she called Pierre at the bistro, at the hour of lunch or dinner, when he was really busy, demanding him to solve yet a new problem she had created. She would not let go of him until he became upset and hung up on her, which recreated the feeling of being abandoned; like she felt her parents did to her when they left her with a foster family.

Simone used to call me frequently to complain about loneliness and her inability to lead a pleasant life. Lengthy and useless conversations.

'Why don't you go away for a few days?' I suggested.

'Because the children need me.'

'The kids are old enough to take care of themselves for a few days and I think they would love to see you go.'

'Maybe you are right,' she answered. 'But, you know, right now I don't have the money to go on a vacation.'

She gave an overview of her financial situation. The lack of income out of Pierre's bistro, how costly the children were, that she had just promised them a European vacation.

'So come stay with us for a few days,' I suggested. If travel is a problem we'll pay for the ticket.'

I thought that I had solved the problem.

'Let me think about it, I'll call you right back,' she hesitated.

She did. On her behalf, I booked flights that I had to change three times because she kept altering her itinerary.

Finally she called to cancel her trip. She found it unfair to go on vacation while Pierre was working.

'He couldn't care less,' I argued. 'He works at his restaurant, has an apartment next door and hasn't been home for months. He probably won't even notice that you're gone as long as you keep disturbing him by phone.'

'Maybe, but then I'll feel guilty.' Again, a lengthy explanation followed about her feelings of guilt and misfortune.

After too many of these kinds of time consuming conversations, I allowed her to call only once a week. As soon as I recognized her voice I started to play a silly computer game or clean out a drawer. My only part in the conversation was: 'Is that so?' every now and then, or, 'life isn't fair.'

She was an impossible woman, permanently damaged by the war and sexual abuse. Alone in this world and unable to gain the power to go on with her life. That was the only reason Pierre didn't divorce her and financially supported her. I even sympathized with her.

There was not much left of the marriage or a family life. Pierre's friends didn't want to visit anymore. Simone interrupted too often and had imposed too many rules. They were no longer allowed to smoke in the house and Simone asked them to lift their feet so she could vacuum while they tried to talk. Pierre finally moved into an apartment next to his restaurant, where he could work, read, listen to music and see his friends who had been banned from his home. Simone and Pierre lived like a divorced couple.

The children quickly learned how to take advantage of this situation in a sly way. Simone promised one of them a new car. Pierre disagreed.

They were arguing on the phone while dinner guests were waiting to be seated. Once, when he could not get rid of her he gave the telephone to me and asked, 'Could you please try to explain to this lovely woman, in English, French, Yiddish, Hebrew or sign language that you cannot spend half a million a year when one only makes a hundred thousand?'

Simone took it in good spirits and started to laugh.

The following day Pierre bought the car that the child had demanded. Her mission was accomplished.

Pierre got to know my parents when they came to visit after Daisy and I had moved from Connecticut to Brentwood. I told him in advance that they were no easy customers.

Pierre calmly explained to me that after being 25 years in business he could handle any situation and told me not to worry.

'This beats any previous situation,' I warned him. 'I bet you two cinema tickets that I am right. No matter who wins, we'll go together and you'll get to see the movie from the start. It's just for the record.'

Pierre accepted my bet.

Several days later Daisy and I took my parents out to dinner to his bistro. At my request he reserved a table in a quiet area. As instructed he lowered the volume of the background music.

Pierre had made notes about my parents' eating habits. No seafood, garlic, pepper or baked potatoes. Only dishes like pot roast with mashed potatoes and overcooked vegetables, because my father thought that he was suffering from an ulcer, caused by his mothers' poor cooking and the lack of food during the war. As a child he told me that I had one too and made my mother put me on a strict diet, only for me to discover later that I was totally healthy and could eat anything I wanted.

As we sat down to have dinner, my mother took Pierre aside and gave him a long list with instructions on how to cook my father's meal. He patiently listened, wrote everything down and offered us a drink.

'We drink with dinner, not before,' my father snapped at him. 'That's why I came to a restaurant. Because I am hungry. It's much too late for dinner already. Now I have a stomach ache. But nobody seems to care.'

'Let me get you some soup,' Pierre responded. 'That's soft on your stomach and ready to serve. Especially prepared for you, like at home.'

After he did, my father tasted a spoonful, made a wry face and complained: 'This soup is cold.'

My mother looked shocked as she had just been bitten by a poisonous snake.

'Is your soup cold, darling? Mine is okay. How is yours?' she asked Daisy and me.

'Mine is fine,' Daisy responded and continued eating.

My father exploded in anger.

'Is it your desire to make a fool of me?' he yelled at Daisy. 'Do you try to publicly insult me or what else is going on in your mind? You may think that I am old, stupid and retarded, that I need someone else to explain what I observe or taste. You women are all alike. You always think that you know everything better. I really don't understand why my own son was ever attracted to you. But that was his poor choice. Nice taste he has.'

My mother tasted his soup and concluded, 'He is right, his soup is not very hot.'

'Cold you mean,' he snapped at her.

'Actually you are right. Your soup is cold.'

Pierre interfered in a tactical manner. He apologized and offered him a new bowl. It came within seconds. Steaming hot. My father tasted again, made a face as if someone had served him worms.

'Now there is garlic in my soup!' he yelled

Pierre assured him that there was no garlic in his soup but that he would be happy to serve him yet another bowl.

'Now you put pepper in my soup,' he complained after the third bowl was served.

He finally ate the fourth bowl with an aggravated expression on his face. Meanwhile my mother talked to him as if she was pampering a little child.

'Don't you worry darling, tomorrow I'll cook for you, exactly the way you like it. I know this isn't right for you but I don't think they do it on purpose.'

Pierre, still holding strong, served the pot roast I had asked for, overcooked and all.

'I have to admit that the meat isn't bad,' my father said after the first taste as he reached for the mustard. He smelled the mustard several times, sticking his nose in the jar, sniffing loudly. He looked disgusted.

'They even put garlic in the mustard,' he complained.

All of Pierre's customers were staring at us.

He came to explain that there was absolutely no garlic in the mustard. He imported the same one for 25 years from a reliable supplier in France.

'Are you implicating that I am a liar?' my father yelled. 'Do you have mustard in your purse?' he asked my mother.

She nervously started to search her large purse that contained all emergency supplies for possible needs my father couldn't live without while on a trip. Sugar, Sweet & Low, instant coffee, powdered milk, crackers and cheese, candies, a sewing kit, a first-aid-kit as well as an impressive collection of pills. A complete mobile pharmacy. There was a pill for everything prescribed by an understanding doctor who could never do anything right in their opinion. Each diagnosis was checked with a medical encyclopedia at home, only to state that the "quack" had been wrong again.

When my mother got hospitalized for a minor illness, a friendly young woman served tea and soft drinks during visiting hour.
'I don't want tea, I want coffee,' my mother complained.
'I am sorry madam, we don't have that right now. If you are willing to wait for fifteen minutes I'll be off duty and I'll be more than happy to brew some fresh for you.'
My father jumped from his seat.
'For all the money you are charging us you refuse to even serve a cup of coffee? Is that too much to ask for a thousand dollars a day? Now I understand why there are so many, so-called unemployed. It's not that there are no jobs available but young people like yourself refuse to work. And then it comes as a so-called surprise when you are laid off? If you are too lazy to serve a simple cup of coffee, I'll fix it myself. How is that?'
'I'm sorry I aggravated you so much,' the woman said patiently. 'But that would be against regulations. Honestly, it won't take me more than fifteen minutes to fix your wife a cup of coffee.'
'I don't need your favors,' he snapped. 'I'll go home, do it myself and bring it in a thermos.'
He angrily left the room, talking to himself about spoiled, young people who were not willing to stick out a finger to help an older person. His anger equaled his rage at Pierre's bistro.

At Café Montmartre we now were facing a serious "mustard crisis." My mother had failed to put any mustard in her purse prior to the flight from Amsterdam to Los Angeles. My father would not easily forgive her this sin. He looked at her with a disapproving expression. She apologized several times.

'I'm very sorry darling. I must have forgotten or lost it. If you want me to, I can go to a McDonald's and get you some there.'

No, he did not want that. He ate his food, silently, with a furious expression. His day was spoiled.

After dinner Pierre offered espresso, a glass of good *cognac* and New York cheesecake.

'Are you putting me on?' my father asked Pierre.

'That filthy German crap. Are you satisfied now? My meal is spoiled. By the way, the music is too loud, it's noisy here.'

'I didn't want to mention it,' my mother immediately supported him in an attempt to calm him down. 'It bothers me too. There is too much noise here. You can hardly hear each other when you talk. You have to yell to hear each other.'

To prove her point she raised her voice so loud that again the other guests were staring at us, exchanging sneering remarks. Pierre had a desperate look on his sweating face, serving espresso's.

My father lit a pipe, creating a cloud of smoke blown into the restaurant. A waitress informed him that smoking was prohibited.

'Now it's enough, I am out of here,' he snarled at her.

He walked outside, slamming the front door. My mother, Daisy and I followed a little later. My father was standing outside in the pouring rain, smoking his pipe. Having it his way.

When we drove home my mother said that she had enjoyed the evening and liked Pierre.

'He is not a cook but a crook,' my father responded. 'He cheated on the bill too,' he blamed me. 'You have always selected the wrong friends. That's the only thing that you are good at.'

Before we went to bed Daisy took a long shower. Once in bed she stared at me and asked, 'How come you are so nice?'

'Maybe they are nice too but sometimes it's hard to discover.'

'I guess so,' she said. 'But one thing. Never ever do I want to be seen with these people in public again. It is so embarrassing. The last time we went out to dinner I returned to offer my apologies to the waiter and gave him an extra tip. But after what they have done to Pierre I've had it. I kept my mouth shut but it wasn't easy.'

'I know all about it, Daisy. However, I can't get angry with them. They survived the Holocaust on the outside. The inside was nearly destroyed, which shows on the outside. Not very pleasant but what can I do? I could be angry with Adolf Hitler but he no longer has a customer service to take complaints. Besides, I earned two movie tickets tonight.'

Daisy switched the lights off; we relaxed into each other's arms and fell asleep.

Now at Café Montmartre, several years later, it felt comfortable sharing a table with Pierre. We enjoyed dinner and with an excellent wine we flushed away the bad taste left behind by visiting Tina and Carl.

It was my father's birthday. Pierre let me use his office to make a phone call to him.

'We are about to leave for Belgium to celebrate my eightieth birthday in an old castle,' he explained. 'I considered inviting you too, but that would only spoil the party for your mother. She cries every night about you because you are wasting your life, traveling around without plans. First you refused to learn, now you refuse to work. You are also unable to love or be loved so you are a sociopath, just like your brother.'

He hung up, failing to thank me for the present I had sent. I smiled. This was the way we communicated.

'At least some things in life are predictable,' I said to Pierre as I returned to our table.

'How are your parents?' he asked.

'Healthy and cheerful as always,' I answered.

'Sure,' said Pierre, giving me the finger. He poured two glasses of the *calvados* that Daisy and I used to have as an after dinner drink. He had ordered a bottle especially for me. He lifted his glass and said, 'Let's drink to the present. The past is behind us, the future unknown. All we know is that we are having a great time together now.' He smiled sadly.

'Cheers to new, good memories for the future,' I toasted.

10

I stayed in southern California for a while. Providing you have money and you are healthy, you don't have to work and fight traffic every day; it's a nice, relaxing area with a good climate. Greater Los Angeles has decayed into an intolerant conglomerate of ethnic islands. Not a real city. People are friendly if they don't cheat or kill one another. To me, European, southern California is a "Wonderworld," secluded from the real world. Those who have bad luck are in the streets, if you sell enough paperwork, business plans or real estate and ignore all surrounding misery, it is an awesome resort. An alternative paradise and a nice contrast to some northern European countries where people are too serious and dull.

Police are the exception. I'll never ever get used to policemen who act like judges and decide whom to harass, beat people up and have conspiracies on which colleagues to back or not. An intolerable abuse of power but the white majority seems to agree. That's why it won't change.

Early in the summer I received a call from Max, a friend from the past. As children we met every Sunday at our clubhouse of Ichud Habonim, a worldwide Zionist youth organization.

Both in summer and winter there were holiday camps, usually in a small village in a forest where children from all over Holland and abroad gathered. We learned about the history of Palestine and Israel, discussed politics, talked about emigration. But most of all it was a meeting place for Jewish children, without exclusion of children of Holocaust survivors.

Their families were all dysfunctional, their homes contaminated with grief and anxiety. The Habonim clubhouse was a safe haven of loyalty between nice kids.

Also to me it was a peaceful shelter with nice, caring people and most importantly, fun was allowed. At home fun was only tolerated if initiated by my father and approved by my mother. My father would make plans to go to a movie sometimes but always added, 'I have to get permission from the highest authorities.'

That was a joke and it wasn't. He took my mother into the kitchen and closed the door. They deliberated like a jury in a courthouse. My brother and I waited for the verdict.

My father was spokesman for the jury. When he came out, there were two possibilities. Or, 'I talked to your mother and she gave me permission,' or 'your mother rightfully says that we can use our money for more useful matters.'

Useful was an important phrase. Books and toys were carefully inspected by the parental consumer forum. Only if they were useful, were they purchased. Stuffed animals for example were not educational and thus not useful. For his seventh birthday my brother desired a radio because he loved music. How many times did we pray for a hung jury? It never happened. This time it was a matter of minutes before my brother received his educational lesson.

'I talked to your mother and she rightfully says that there are more useful ways to spend our money. Go do your homework instead of wasting your time, listening to that awful modern music. That doesn't teach you anything good.'

An "appeal" was out of the question in that dictatorship. The Supreme Court had already judged.

My poor brother decided to join "the resistance." With a little help of an older friend he bought a cheap build-it-yourself crystal receiver, a primitive post war kind of walkman. To receive a station he had to patiently pinch a crystal with a needle at random, until he finally heard the sound of a radio station on his headphones that he had bought at an army surplus store. At night he could secretly listen to his "radio," underneath his blanket. It was his only uncensored contact with the outside world. Until his "crime" was discovered during an unexpected parental nightly inspection. His "illegal receiver" was confiscated. The next day he had to face the jury. The deliberations in the kitchen took over an hour until my father came out with the verdict.

'I discussed it with your mother who rightfully says that you have secretly wasted your pocket money on junk that doesn't belong in this house. Since you were aware of our opinion beforehand, we have concluded that it doesn't make sense to give you pocket money.' As of that day his allowance was cut off.

A week later a request by Eric and me to buy a soccer ball was turned down.

"I discussed it with your mother who rightfully says that soccer is a game for goyim, not for Jews.'

At Habonim meetings, fun was one of the main ingredients. No questions were asked if something was useful or educational. Most of the plans we made could be realized.

Participation with the organization had been approved by the "jury" at home because I had thrown in the educational aspects. This forced me into covering for this statement by reading as much as I could about Israel and its history. Every time I returned from a meeting my father tested me on what it was we learned.

'It's inaccurate, but what do kids nowadays know,' he concluded each week.

Max was a few years younger than I. We called each other *Partners in Crime*, friends through thick and thin. As a child he moved to Washington D.C. where his father had a high position at the World Bank. We stayed in touch. I was privileged to be best man when he married Gaby, an extremely sweet woman. They raised a son, David, in a beautiful house in Brooklyn Heights, overlooking the New York harbor and the Statue of Liberty. Max made a good living as the CFO of an airline. Gaby held a job as a chemistry teacher at a local college. She enjoyed her work and her pupils.

Shortly after the shiva, Max wrote me a lengthy letter inviting me to David's Bar Mitzvah, in November. At the time I didn't feel like joining a party without Daisy. I kept running into people who did not know what had happened, asking me how Daisy was doing, forcing me to tell the same story over and over again. That way I kept painfully running into myself.

Now Max called to say that he had made big plans for his son's Bar Mitzvah. He invited seven or eight *Partners in Crime*, our old childhood clubhouse friends. They were living all over the world and Max had offered to pay for airline tickets and hotel.

'You have to come too,' he insisted. 'Everybody is asking how you are and told me to say hello to you. I told all the guests you know about Daisy's death, so you don't have to worry about tactless questions and you won't be alone.'

Listening to him, the thought became appealing. The idea of a reunion with the *Partners in Crime* made me feel comfortable. A chance of a lifetime to get together once more, which would not likely happen again. It would also be a nice opportunity for me to see my brother Eric in New York, so I gratefully accepted Max's invitation.

'I pay my own bills,' I insisted. 'It is a mitzvah to witness the Bar Mitzvah of your son.'

11

Two days before David's Bar Mitzvah I checked into the hotel where the other *Partners in Crime* would stay. I wanted to be present prior to their arrival. Fred, Michael, Phil and Sally arrived late in the afternoon from Amsterdam. Mony, Rachel and Esther travelled a day later from Tel Aviv, Rachel from Cyprus and Dave and Leslie from San Francisco.

I comfortably settled myself at a strategically located table where I could keep an eye on the reception desk. Some of my *Partners in Crime* I had not seen for years or decades. I wondered if I would still recognize them. I didn't have to wait long.

It was like time had stood still. Fred had gained some weight and lost most of his hair, but the expression in his funny eyes had not changed a bit, still looking mischievous. Michael was still a drunk and had the biggest mouth. Phil was helping Sally. She was crippled by arthritis, walked with crutches. Her body was severely deformed but her face still radiated love and happiness.

Fred was "the comedian." During our weekly gatherings he entertained the group with funny songs he wrote. He looked exactly like his father who used to run a cheap clothing store out of his home together with his wife a colossal woman who, without any doubt, was the boss of the business as well as the family. No one would think of arguing with her, except Fred. However, even when Fred was in his late forties, she would discipline him.

'Today I was in a department store,' she babbled. 'Oy, there was such a sweet little toddler. I wanted to hug him but as I approached he started to cry.'

'I would panic too, if I was about to be crunched by a steamroller,' Fred reacted. A split second later he received two hard slaps on his cheek. No fooling around with "mama." That was clear.

Fred's father fled from Poland, via Germany and Holland to Belgium, in an attempt to remain out of the hands of the Nazis. He succeeded thanks to his gift of unlimited chutzpah and coincidences. In 1943 he was arrested in Belgium and put on the train to Auschwitz. The steam locomotive pulled thirty goods wagons, carrying 1638 prisoners and a passenger car for the German soldiers. A small resistance group managed to stop the train. They put a red light between the tracks that looked like a red sign. When the train stopped they held the engine-driver at gunpoint and opened several wagons. They yelled at the prisoners to get out. Many of them didn't,from fear of being caught. 231 escaped. 23 were killed by German bullets. Fred's father was one of the lucky ones. His liberators gave him some money and he quickly found a hiding place where he became claustrophobic after a while. He left his hiding place to take a walk. His fellows in hiding objected, but he decided to challenge the danger. He was arrested by the SS and taken to their local headquarters for questioning. He knew that the SS could force him to disclose his hiding place. All of the others would be transported to one of the destruction camps. He was not carrying the yellow star of David with the word "Jew" on it, which was mandatory and he had a fake identity card of less than mediocre quality.

A young officer tried to ask him some questions. Instead of answering, he started to behave like an upset, wealthy customer of an expensive store.

'Do you think that you are going to get away with this?' he said in fluent German. 'You don't seem to realize whom you are dealing with. I won't talk to you, young man. I demand to speak to your highest superior, immediately.'

The officer hit him.

'Eventually everybody answers my questions,' he said. 'I have my methods.'

Fred's father jumped up, standing nose to nose with the officer, like a drill sergeant.

'You are burning your bridges,' he yelled into the face of the SS officer. 'I will talk to your superiors with or without your assistance and I will not recommend you for a promotion. Until now you have had an easy office job, but they also need soldiers in the field, bleeding and freezing to death in the Russian snow. Got that?'

On and on he went, intimidating the officer until he really talked his way into the commander's office.

Before he could open his mouth the man commanded: 'Close the door, sit down and shut up, Dreckjude. Play with fire and you'll get burned.'

He stared at Fred's father with an unfathomable expression on his face. A long threatening silence. Minutes felt like hours.

Suddenly he leaned forward.

'Do you see the door behind me?' he whispered. 'Behind that door are fire stairs. Go out that door now, go home and for God's sake make sure that you never cross my men's path again.'

After giving his orders, the commander ignored Fred's father and started to sign documents as if nothing had happened.

Fred's father climbed down the fire stairs and ran home because he couldn't wait to share his heroic behavior with the other fourteen men and women who were hiding in the same place. As he came home, he discovered the house was empty. One of the neighbors had betrayed them. They were arrested to be deported to Auschwitz.

'They were arrested while I was in the safest place in the city,' he told us, showing his feelings of guilt as well as his courageous bravura. 'I was sitting at the SS commanders' office and talked myself out of there.'

Fred was a talented writer, played the guitar and piano and was a good singer. As a comedian his humor was blunt and shameless. He didn't care about the feelings of his audience. Usually he was funny. He was gifted enough to make it big as a professional entertainer. But somehow, each time he came close to success, he blew it.

He told me that he got a sexual kick out of danger. It started during early childhood. He was on a swing, his mother had told him not to go up too high, which he purposely did anyway. As he came dangerously close to falling ten feet, upside down, his mother screamed hysterically. It generated a wonderful feeling, as he described his first orgasm.

Via friends in the entertainment industry, we arranged for a couple of television performances for him. Live broadcasting. He wrote two new songs and both times, during the performance he forgot the words. He had not rehearsed enough and could not read the cue cards because he had left his glasses in the dressing room.

At important business meetings, like with record companies that showed interest in his work, he usually showed up late or not at all. When he got an offer from an Amsterdam theater to perform for two months, he left for Spain "to prepare himself." He returned two weeks after "his première." He cancelled performances at the last moment, telling tales about migraine attacks and went to a pub instead to perform there. He really didn't care what people thought about his unreliability. He still got a kick out of tension. After several of these experiences none of us wanted to get involved anymore with his dream to become a professional entertainer. In spite of this all, we tolerated him.

He married a woman twice as big and three times as loud. She created a strict regime for him after the occurrence of some rather upsetting incidents.

When his wife asked him to take care of their two little sons, instead of taking them to school he reported them ill and took them out to the zoo. Until today he doesn't realize why his wife became angry with him.

To earn a living he became a social worker in a penitentiary. It was a short career because he virtually violated all the rules, leaving prisoners and their visiting spouses unattended "so they could enjoy some privacy." He ignored complaints from the prison guards and almost got fired. He got suspended and a psychological evaluation was ordered. The psychologist mildly formulated in his report that Fred didn't accept any authority from superiors. Colleagues at the same level or below did not accept him. Nonetheless, a forgiving supervisor in the personell department gave him one more chance, on probation, at a lower security institution. Four days after he was supposed to start working there, he called me for advice. He had "forgotten" to show up at his new job. I advised him to call his new boss and ask if he was still welcome. He thanked me kindly and promised to follow my advice immediately. Instead he called in sick. That night someone from the personell department ran into him, playing songs in a crowded pub. He was fired on the spot.

Even though he had no more income, he kept spending big, until his wife, who was wealthy, rationed him. She took his credit cards, bank card and gave him one hundred dollars pocket money per week, no matter what.

Michael was a tall, happy guy who often was in trouble, because he liked to help his friends and spent much more on them than he could afford. After his parents' antique store was no longer profitable he bought them a hardware store, including all the inventory. This was of course way beyond his reach. Fortunately his parents-in-law were well to do and bailed him out of trouble several times. Michael had a successful dental practice. Once in a while he got the urge to go overboard and use every credit card to the limit.

When Michael ran into Fred earlier that day at the Amsterdam airport, he immediately asked Fred how much pocket money his "mommy" had given him to go on his trip to New York. With a funny smile Fred took his wallet out of his pocket and showed Michael a one hundred dollar bill.

Michael didn't hesitate, grabbed the hundred dollars, ran straight into the duty free store and came back carrying two big yellow shopping bags filled with good scotch and cigarettes.

'Here is your change,' he said to Fred and gave him a few nickels and dimes. Fred was speechless and Michael left him like that until they landed in New York where he handed Fred a thousand dollars.

'Now you don't have to constantly sponge us, like you usually do,' he added.

'That's more like it,' said Fred. 'Let's stop at a good delicatessen so we can build a little party tonight.'

He ordered the taxi driver to stop at a well-known exorbitantly expensive store. He and Michael went in. Fred loaded two big shopping carts with excess wines, liquor, snacks and cheeses; enough for a good size cold buffet. When they reached the cashier, Fred told Michael he was going to open the trunk of the car, leaving the unpaid bill for Michael.

Sally was the oldest of the group. She had been our Habonim clubhouse teacher on the history of Jews in the Diaspora, Zionism, Judaism and the Middle East. She used to be a pretty girl but arthritis had taken its toll. She could hardly walk or sit straight, was constantly in pain, had a few joints replaced and still had several operations to go. Her brother, younger by two years, had died of bone cancer during his last year in high school. Still Sally was a cheerful and happy woman who loved her teaching job.

Phil we nicknamed "The Compiler" because of the tremendous number of women he dated. He was unable to stay in a relationship. He grew up with his mother after his father had been hospitalized in a mental institution, psychically and mentally ruined in a concentration camp.

His mother had no idea how to handle the situation. She was young and inexperienced, born in 1936. She lost her parents during the war. She had never known family life, had hardly known her parents, and was hidden in a monastery where she got little education. There she grew up without affection. At age sixteen she married. Not so much out of love, but he was the only man she knew and had socialized with. Three years later he was hospitalized and died shortly afterward. Phil did not remember his father at all.

His mother created devastating chaos in the house. No one could find anything without digging through old newspapers, books, dirty laundry or garbage that was scattered around everywhere. When she received her monthly benefit from the government she spent it right away on things they didn't need.

We used to give Phil sandwiches at our weekly meetings, because we knew he often had not been fed for several days. Sometimes he was wearing wet clothes because his mother had forgotten to dry them after washing.

He did anything possible to try and please his mother, but he could never meet her expectations that were unrealistically high.

Phil became a reporter with a local television station. If his mother ran into a neighbor or an acquaintance, she said: 'Did you see Phil on television yesterday? I am so proud. He is very famous now, thanks to everything I have managed to do for him, which was not easy.'

Phil himself never got any credit from her. He tried as best as he could to please her and to get some recognition from her, but to no avail.

The first evening with Fred, Michael, Sally and Phil was relatively quiet. We exchanged a few travel experiences and amusing stories.

The only incident was set off by Fred and Phil. In a corner section of the dining room a wedding dinner was in progress. Fred looked at Phil and without exchanging a word, Phil got up and asked for the master of ceremonies.

'The entertainment has arrived,' he told the man who obviously had no idea what Phil was talking about. Before the master of ceremonies could say anything Phil continued: 'After the main dish, as agreed upon, the waiters must stop service during the performance. And he does twenty minutes maximum. By the way, I already received a check from uncle... what's his name? Nice surprise for the family, don't you think? But keep your lips sealed, good man, because a surprise is a surprise.'

Fred had picked up his guitar from his room and half an hour later he did an excellent show, made everybody laugh, even found out some names of family members so he could personalize his jokes. Phil instructed the photographer to take as many pictures as possible. After the performance we ordered after dinner drinks and desserts in an adjoining lounge, to listen in to the conversations at the wedding dinner. All the guests questioned one another, but of course nobody admitted to have ordered the entertainment. Two men even got into an argument about it.

Fred, Michael and Sally retired to their rooms, after a long day of travel. Phil stayed. He obviously had made eye contact with an attractive lady at the bar and was ready for "another one for the road."

The next day Esther, Rachel and Mony arrived.

Mony was the only one of us who really knew for sure as a child that he wanted to emigrate to Israel. He went at age eighteen to join an elite unit of the Israeli army. He left with a broken heart, leaving his much younger sister in the care of his parents who had been victims of Mengele's medical experiments in Auschwitz. They had scars all over their bodies, his dad had several fingers and toes missing.

Shortly after Mony joined the Israeli army his father died of a massive heart attack. His mother passed away under mysterious circumstances. Most likely she committed suicide.

His little sister was an orphan at age sixteen. There was not much he could do for her, except give her a little financial support and contact a friend who let her live in his house.

From a distance he watched her suffering. She stayed inside her new home for a year, primarily sleeping and became isolated and unfriendly. She finally decided to emigrate to Israel too, but was unable to find work or establish long lasting relationships or friendships. Not even with Mony, because she felt abandoned by him. A pretty, bright young woman who was unable to enjoy life. Several psychologists and psychiatrists were unable to help her get back on track. Full of fear, she kept sheltering from the world. She never dressed in a flattering way, thinking she was ugly, couldn't show joy or anger and her sexual desires had vanished. She couldn't take care of herself and would not allow others to support her. Her only acquaintances were women of her deceased mother's age. She became furious when Mony talked about her "surrogate mothers."

Mony became a well-respected writer, married Yael, an Israeli woman who gave him two children and a stable life. I could not remember one occasion when he was laughing. He had been exposed to an overdose of cruel stories. He could not understand why his mother wanted children and committed suicide, leaving him with his little sister whom he had been unable to comfort and who was angry with him.

Esther was born in 1938, in the Dutch Indies. She grew up in several Japanese concentration camps where she and her mother were tortured and constantly humiliated.

She had a big scar on her left underarm. As a small girl she had tried to steal some food from the kitchen. A cook caught her "in action," transfixed her arm with a meat hook and hung her between the carcasses of goats, the food for the guards. The prisoners got practically nothing. A small ration of rice. Many of them died due to malnutrition, lack of medical care and severe torture.

Esther was forced to whip her mother who was accused of "conspiracy." She was forced down on her knees, because the Japanese guards refused "to look up" to their victims. Her mother whispered to Esther to obey the guard's orders and did not make a sound during the torture, to make her daughter believe that it did not hurt. The guards forced her to hit hard.

Esther's mother barely survived the Japanese terror. Her father was a slave laborer at the feared Burma Railroad. He did survive, but when he finally returned to Holland he was unrecognizable. The children accepted his presence but did not communicate. The Dutch who returned from Japanese occupation in the Dutch Indies, a former Dutch colony, did not receive any assistance or recognition from the Dutch government for a lengthy period of time. Only when it was too late.

'Just a leaflet from the former queen, that she was proud of us,' Esther once told me. The Dutch government was totally indifferent to the victims of the cruelties of the Japanese occupier. Even today they still fight for recognition and financial compensation. The Dutch government doesn't seem to care and the Japanese authorities - unlike the German government - never admitted guilt and refused to provide reparations.

Esther's brother committed suicide. Esther carried on. Sad and lonely. Her wounds did not heal and only became more severe as she aged.

She was vacationing in Israel and decided to join Mony on his trip to New York for the small "reunion."

Rachel's story is bizarre. She arrived from Cyprus where she met her two sons. She had no connection to *The Partners in Crime*, until she was an adult. She was the only daughter of a religious fundamentalist family. At age seventeen a "match" was made for her. Shortly afterward the chupah took place. It was clear that she had no choice. If she had ran away she would have been totally cut off by the family and the small ultra-orthodox community. Outside that society she knew no one. She was like a prisoner. No freedom, no money, no way to get in touch with the outside world. She was forced to marry Isaac, a disgusting, smelly young creature with unhealthy skin, bad breath and a downy beard. He was dressed in the prehistoric costume that originated in Eastern Europe. A long black coat, worn-out black slacks with shiny, greasy spots where he rested his hands during his endless studies of the Talmud. His big black hat made him look like Amish. He did not do anything else but study religious books, pray and discuss the holy writings. His wealthy parents supported his "sit and learn" lifestyle. Rachel described him as the most unattractive, dirty young man on earth. He hardly gave her money for food or clothing. She walked around in rags, covering her body from neck to ankles, a cheap wig, covering her pretty hair and a hat to show to the outside world that she was married.

Once a month, on the eighth day after her period and her monthly visit to the mikva, Isaac covered all "holy books" with towels and table clothes, then ordered her to take off her girdle and slip and raped her.

Phil ran into Isaac and Rachel at a reception. When Isaac got deeply involved in a discussion with his friends, Rachel took her chances by quickly turning to Phil, hoping that he would be trustworthy. She quickly explained her situation and begged him to help her. He didn't hesitate at all.

He phoned me to confer.

'Call the other *Partners in Crime*,' I advised. 'We all have to make a contribution so she can rent an apartment and pay her bills until she finds a job.'

Dave advanced the entire amount needed. A week later, when Rachel picked her two boys up from school, Phil was there. He drove them to a new, sunny apartment complex, protected by a security guard. Dave had comfortably decorated the apartment and bought toys for the children. They immediately started to enjoy this luxury of happiness and freedom. Phil told Rachel under no circumstances to allow Isaac to see the boys unsupervised.

Rachel adjusted fast and well to her new situation. After three months she found a teaching job and lived comfortably, with a little help from her new *Partners in Crime*.

After four months of peaceful existence Isaac suddenly made his appearance. Via the security guard he asked if he could see the children for a minute. He had bought them some presents for the holidays.

Rachel accompanied her children downstairs. The children were excited to see their dad and took a run at him. He grabbed them by the arm, pushed them in a chauffeured car and kidnapped them to Jerusalem and later to the Jewish settlement in Hebron. The kids spent their time inside, being brainwashed with political issues and religion. Sometimes Rachel got to see them for a few hours in Cyprus, guarded by fundamentalist community members of her ex-husband. They looked like miniature copies of their father. Pale, dressed in worn-out black suits and wearing dark hats, as if the Almighty had ordered these uniforms in Israel's hot climate.

Rachel twice approached the Israeli Rabbinate, because her children were kidnapped. Both times she was told that "perhaps her case could be reviewed, in exchange for a reasonable donation." Not a "bribe" but "for your cooperation you have my gratitude," as Oscar Schindler is quoted so many times, dealing of course with a totally different kind of mafia of power and corruption.

Mony, who was a generous contributor to Rachel's escape from her husband, witnessed it all happen; the uphill battle of Rachel trying to get her children back from Israel. He lost a great deal of faith in the Jewish State for which he had sacrificed quite a bit.

On top of that his son met a girl from Holland, Brigitte. She presented herself as a second generation victim of the Holocaust. She appeared to be an attractive, likable young lady. Her life hadn't been easy, according to her stories. Her parents had assimilated, denied their Judaism. She left home at a young age to search for her roots. To learn more about Judaism she spent a year with a religious family in Antwerp, she told Mony's son. A sad but endearing story. She got pregnant from Mony's son after two months. The two had a chupah after which it was discovered that she was a fraud who had emigrated to Israel on falsified documents. On her identity card it showed that she was Jewish, but the Amsterdam Jewish community wrote a statement that the document used, on their letterhead, was forged. The justice department, the Rabbinate and Ministry of Immigration refused to provide any kind of help.

After her false identity was discovered and it became obvious that her résumé had been totally fantasized, she reported Mony's son several times to the police for alleged abuse. He was arrested and went through lengthy and costly trials. Meanwhile he received a restraining order. He could no longer enter his own house. Brigitte took the opportunity during his absence to steal all of his belongings and strip his bank accounts. Police refused to accept his complaints, because the officers did not want to get involved in "a domestic argument." Awaiting the divorce trial - that took seven years at the Rabbinical Court and Family Court - he was not allowed to leave the country. The judgments of the two Courts contradicted. In the end she was not convicted of forgery or theft. The civil judge – who was clearly not interested in the case – didn't even force her to return the stolen goods and money. He decided that the child was Jewish and thus the mother too. The Israeli justice system sometimes is not very sophisticated, to put it mildly.

That's how this Christian, European woman managed to get the protection of Israel's law. By the time everyone she knew discovered that she was a pathological liar, she disappeared to Holland with Mony's granddaughter, leaving debts everywhere that Mony's son had to pay and which left him with "bad credit." All of his letters to the authorities remained unanswered.

A country without separation of church and state brings injustice. A theocracy leaves little space for real democracy and justice. But worst of all, Mony was disappointed because the bureaucracy did not seem to care, in fact tried to encourage his son to quit writing and protesting.

As Mony phrased it: 'If Herzl were still alive he would turn around in his grave.' Brigitte, as an "Israeli Jew" talked her way into a small, local Dutch Jewish Community and lied herself into a job with a social housing project, once more with a forged résumé. As a bisexual she was able to charm men and women alike. She became president of the Dutch branch office of Keren Hayesod, United Israel Appeal. All based on lies, until the past caught up with her and she was laid off.

12

At five o'clock Esther came to see me in my room. She had a cast on her wrist.

I asked her what happened.

'Just a little accident a couple of weeks ago,' she answered.

'Did you break it?'

'Yes.'

'How?'

She blushed. 'I punched somebody in the face,' she said.

'How did that happen?'

'It happened before I realized it myself,' she explained. 'I am so ashamed. I never hurt anyone in my life and now I hit a teenager, real hard.'

'You must have had a good reason?'

'I visited a huge art fair in the center of town, with a friend. Most of the people were just out having a good time. But there was a group of skinheads. Leather jackets, swastikas and all, looking for trouble. We tried to avoid them but we couldn't move fast enough in the big crowd. One of these kids had a bicycle chain in his hand. Just to upset people he swung it around. It hit me, but not real hard. I decided to try and ignore him but then he hit me again and yelled: "Move, you fucking whore." Before I realized what I was doing I hit him right in the mouth, as hard as I could. I heard his bones crack, broke his nose and knocked out a number of teeth. He fell down, bleeding like hell. I couldn't believe what I had done. The people in the crowd applauded, but I felt terrible. Later I noticed that my wrist was hurting so I went to the emergency room. While I was waiting for a doctor I wondered why I did this. What puzzled me too was that I didn't get angry when he hit me with that chain, but I went totally out of control when he used that dirty language. Why? And why, before I started to feel bad about what I had done, for a split second I felt a big sigh of relief? A liberating feeling. Did I enjoy hitting a child? It was scary, the thought that I could hurt someone before I could realize it and then felt good about it for a moment.'

'So what shall we call you from now on?' I asked. "Esther the terrible, the butcher of Amsterdam?" I sympathize with that crowd. The dipstick deserved it. I don't admire your exterminator style, but he attacked you so you had the right to defend yourself, without the self punishment of a guilt trip afterwards.'

'I am not talking about guilt,' Esther responded. 'What was eating me was that I enjoyed what I did. I felt good, satisfied.'

'If this is your way of getting satisfaction it's going to be tough to find you a nice partner,' I said.

'I was deeply shocked while I was sitting in that waiting room at the hospital. I didn't even notice my wrist hurting. Suddenly it came to me. When I was a child in these Japanese camps, that's what the guards used to do to us. They had these whips that they kept cracking. I'll never forget that sound. They hit us too, which was extremely painful, but you had to keep your mouth shut to avoid worse. The guards yelled at us. "Move, faster you fucking whores." For some unknown reason we always had to speed it up while there was nothing to do. When you spend several years in a concentration camp you don't mind being a minute early or late. When my mother tried to protect me, they locked her up in a wooden crate or an oil drum, in the burning sun. For days, without water or food. She almost died of exhaustion. All my anger, all these fears. I have never had a chance to talk about it. There was no debriefing team waiting for us after the war, so I shoved it aside and tried to carry on. I released decades of anger in that one hit in the face of that stupid kid. I let it out on somebody else. He didn't deserve that.'

13

'Are you two screwing around in there?' Michael screamed, banging on the door.

I opened the door.

Esther got the giggles when she saw the porter rolling an enormous cart into the room filled with boxes of wine, whisky and food. This "cold buffet" was followed by Michael and a cheerful Fred, carrying his guitar case.

'Aren't we exaggerating a little bit?' Fred asked Michael.

'Don't horse shit me, you parasite,' Michael responded. 'You collected all this stuff in the store, until a certain moment. That store never had better clientele. Until the moment it had to be paid. Then you vanished in the haze like Adolf Eichman after the war. You are the perfect acting moralist, like a preacher on a Christian network, collecting donations. When you talk about good and bad we get tears in our eyes. So tender, straight, justifiable. Like a real Talmudic expert. When food is served you are the loudest smacker, when wine needs to be selected you are the "connoisseur" ordering the most expensive ones; tasting *armagnac* you can tell if it's fifty or sixty years old, but when the bill arrives you disappear like the holy ghost. Suddenly missing in action.'

Michael put his arm on Fred's shoulder.

'Perhaps your mommy keeps you a little tight on your allowance. That is the most diplomatic explanation.'

The porter had unloaded his cart and stored everything in an orderly manner.

'This young, talented millionaire is going to take care of your tip,' Michael said, pointing at Fred.

Fred had no choice but to reach for his wallet, a move he did not seem to enjoy.

'I'm sorry,' he said. 'I only have one hundred dollar bills.'

'Not to worry,' Michael instantly responded. He grabbed two hundred dollars out of Fred's wallet and gave it to the porter.

'Keep the change,' Michael said.

The porter bowed and buoyantly left the room while the other *Partners in Crime* walked into my room.

Phil was accompanied by the woman that he had met in the bar, the evening before. A beauty with dark, friendly eyes.

Sally wanted to make a remark about his new catch but Phil didn't give her the opportunity.

'I am not as bad as my reputation,' he said. 'This is Joan. She lives here. We have known each other for over ten years. Before I left home I called her to ask her to meet me here.'

Joan introduced herself in fluent Dutch. She was a child of an American soldier and a Dutch mother, who got pregnant right after the war. They got married and settled down in the New York area. The marriage did not last long. Joan's father left after a few years, leaving her and her mother in poverty. However, her mother succeeded in giving Joan a happy childhood and a good education.

We had seen Phil with dozens of women. For the first time he looked comfortable and happy.

'Welcome to the *Partners in Crime*,' Mony said. 'As an old and well-established pillar of civilized society, we are always on the search for new members. We voted by ballot and our decision is positive, even though you were introduced by Phil.'

'Now I'll become a senior member,' Rachel said.

'Let sleeping dogs lie, you bag of bones,' said Michael while pouring drinks to the rim for everyone. 'I almost forgot but you silently sneaked in after you ran away from that smelly wanderoo, but never paid your contribution.'

'How much do you want from me?' asked Rachel.

'I don't want your money,' Michael protested. 'I would never do that to you, you poor, vulnerable little thing. That could traumatize your tender soul. No, I am a conscious man. I want your contribution in nature's garb.'

'Retroactively from the day I joined, based on once per week?' Rachel asked. 'In that case we should excuse ourselves immediately. I am a ten year member, so I owe you five hundred and twenty sexual favors. You only have two days to cash in. I'm ready but it's going to be a small problem for you, especially since you are constantly shikker. If you can make it, you won, if not, you owe me. What that is, I will tell you afterward. Well, take it or leave it.'

'That's unfair,' Mony complained. 'He is not our treasurer. Thank God he isn't. The entire world would roll in wealth, except for us. We share responsibilities. Good and bad. To be friendly I place you in the last category. We'll all take advantage of your generous, stylish offer. Get some Viagra.'

'Objection, men's talk,' said Sally. 'Do you simply think that Esther, Joan and I silently agree. We want our share too.'

'In that case I withdraw my generous, ethical proposal,' said Rachel.

'Nothing has changed, all these years,' Michael mumbled. 'Bring us together and in a matter of minutes we are back to the only subject that we always had in common. Zionism? Israel? Comrades? Up yours. No my young men and women. There was only one thing that kept our ideologically orientated group united. The continuous desire for sex.'

There were two loud bangs on the door followed by a man's voice.

'Are you going to be quiet in there or do you want me to call the hotel manager?'

Michael shook a bottle of club soda, his thumb on the spout, opened the door and sprayed Max straight in the face. He was dripping wet.

'Welcome host,' Michael greeted him. 'I just thought that you were the winner of the Tour de France. Sorry about that. We'd like to thank you in advance for picking up the huge bills that we are planning to leave behind.' Then they hugged.

'How have you all been?' said Max. Michael started to dab Max's wet sweater with a towel.

'It's so good to see you,' Max continued. 'Did you recover from your trips?

'No more of that sentimental small talk. Shut up you jackass and drink,' Michael said to Max, pouring him a large water glass with scotch, filled to the rim.

Max stared at it for a moment and then said: 'Oh, what the heck. L'chayim. Welcome to a once-in-a-life-time reunion of the *Partners in Crime*, sponsored by my mother-in-law who wanted this Bar Mitzvah to be more glamorous than the funeral of the Pope, or at least more tacky than the Bar Mitzvah of her neighbors' grandson. Here you go, you old bitch.'

With his eyes closed he emptied his glass.

'Fill it up, sonny,' he said to Michael who responded right away.

'Don't you have to be home the night before David's Bar Mitzvah?' asked Joan.

'Oh, absolutely,' answered Max and emptied his second glass of scotch.

'Aye, aye, Herr Direktor,' said Michael and filled the glass up again.

'I think that you should slow down a little bit here, Max,' Sally said. 'You need to go home soon. We want you to be in good shape tomorrow morning in shul. And so should we all.'

The whole group started booing.

'Did you really think that I came all the way to New York to go to bed at ten?' asked Fred.

'All right, I give up,' said Sally. 'Nothing has changed in all these years. Back then, during our summer and winter camps nobody wanted to go to bed in the evening or get up in the morning.'

'So you should have slept with me,' Michael interrupted. 'Now it's too late.'

'You know what I'll do?' Sally responded. 'Exactly what I always did. Give up and join the party.'

'Now we're talking,' said Fred, putting his hand on her shoulder.

Phil's friend Joan chipped in to the conversation.

'Why don't you play some songs Fred. I never heard them. And maybe a little later it's nice if each of you tell, in a nutshell what you have been doing lately.'

'Oh yes, group therapy,' Michael responded. 'Fred, why don't you start, so we will be through in thirty seconds.'

'You haven't even paid your contribution to me yet to take charge of me and the entire organization,' Phil said to Joan.

'With your track record?' Joan asked. 'Not a chance. First I want to see the results of your HIV tests over the past ten years, then maybe it's your turn, but don't take that for granted.'

Fred tuned his guitar and started to play some nostalgic songs. After the second one Michael interrupted.

'You haven't changed a bit,' he said. 'As long as your audience isn't larger than fifteen people you don't screw up, but if we put you on stage or in front of a camera you go blank.'

It aggravated Fred. He put his guitar in its case.

'Cheer up,' said Michael. 'Here is a bottle of good wine. We like your songs. As long as you sing you don't talk, you see? And when you don't talk, you don't create accidents. I protect you. That's what friends are for.'

The next few hours everybody gave an update on what they had been doing, about their spouses, children and parents.

My turn did not take very long.

'I am a recovering workaholic,' I said. 'I have no news because everybody knows what happened. I lost my wife and now I try to find an acceptable way to live. That's all. I've just learned one thing for sure, nothing is for sure.'

'Or forever,' said Fred. 'I wouldn't be surprised if my marriage would collapse one of these days.'

'Is she finally coming to her senses?' asked Michael.

'That will give her some extra closet space,' Rachel added. 'She'll be happy to trash all of your shabby outfits. Maybe she won't even notice that you're gone, because you have never been there for her anyhow.'

'Easy on the spouses,' Max said. 'I may be the next homeless one if I don't go home soon. I can use my energy better than fighting my wife. She wins anyhow. A waste of energy.'

'Talking about cheap energy,' I said. 'Where are Dave and Leslie?'

'They arrive late tonight,' Max answered. 'Dave had to change his itinerary to attend some business meeting in Hong Kong, or so. Leslie wants to stay in a different hotel, I believe.'

'This one has a presidential suite too,' said Rachel.

'I don't think so,' Max responded. 'He told me that Leslie got cold feet when she learned that we were planning on getting together. Afraid that he would take the phrase *Partners in Crime* too literary and do something stupid again, like stepping in his right mind out of a wrong bed.'

'I like to hear Leslie's version of that story,' said Phil, comfortably lying down on Joan's lap. 'Usually her motives are quite rational. She learned that the hard way after all these years with Dave. Remember that vacation in Switzerland?' he asked me.

When Dave was just married, he had been heavily overspending and two of his investors, who did not know that the other was involved, had coincidentally met. To avoid a confrontation Dave decided to disappear for a short while to join Phil and me for a short ski vacation in Davos, Switzerland.

When we arrived in our hotel room he opened his suitcase and started to curse.

'God damn it, that stupid woman.'

'That's a pleonasm,' Phil responded. 'What happened?'

Dave explained that he had lied at home about his trip. His wife had accused him of irresponsible spending and that she was sick and tired of receiving certified confiscation notes from his debtors. That conversation took place just prior to the moment that he had been planning on telling her that he was about to take a short vacation with his friends in Davos, not the cheapest destination, to say the least. He thus made up a story on the spot. He told her that he had to attend a black tie business event in Paris. She packed his suitcase and now he was stuck with a tuxedo, patent leathers, two tuxedo shirts with bow tie and shiny gold cufflinks with diamonds.

'Perhaps you can find a job as a waiter?' Phil suggested.

He did not even have a warm jacket and had to lean on Phil and me not to fall down on the slippery, icy pavement as we walked to a clothing store. He bought a pile of thermal underwear, a designer ski outfit and matching moon boots.

A glance in a mirror confirmed his satisfaction.

'That's one down,' he smiled. 'Protected against minus forty degrees, ready to climb Mount Everest. On to the athletic side of me.'

He grabbed a pair of ski's approved by a recent Olympic champion and matching shoes, the only pair in his large size.

'A real champ needs an appropriate outfit,' he stated. 'Check please!' He grabbed one-way mirror sunglasses that covered most of his face. He looked like an astronaut.

'You look like a lunatic,' said Phil.

'Maybe,' Dave responded, 'but at least nobody can recognize me now. You guys have to take this stuff home after the vacation, because I don't want Leslie to explode.'

'Why don't you tell her that you had to purchase this protective outfit because there was an outbreak of Veterans Disease at your Paris business gathering?' I asked. 'Or, why don't you just call her to tell her the truth? Now we are involved too.'

That evening he told us that he had talked to his wife and that everything had been resolved. 'She is in good spirits,' he added.

The next morning the phone rang early. I picked it up. Leslie had obtained the phone number via my office.

'Do you know where Dave is?' she asked.

'In case you mean that snoring, smelly bum, who is about to meet today's hangover, the answer is yes,' I replied.

'How nice of him to take you to Paris too,' Leslie responded naively. I passed the phone to Dave, who was still out of it.

'Why don't you describe the wonderful view on the Eiffel Tower?'

I asked and disappeared into the shower. When I came out he said: 'If she asks you anything, tell her that you invited me to come down here for one day.'

I got myself a separate room and asked him not to get me involved again, after which Dave, Phil and I had a fun ski vacation.

'Leslie thought that we encouraged him to do all that nonsense,' Phil said from Joan's lap.

'What do you mean by *we*?' asked Esther. 'It sounds like a group, a conspiracy, the cell of an illegal movement. There is only one reason we ever got together.'

'Sex,' was Michael's immediate conclusion.

'We wanted to emigrate to Israel. Only Mony did. Great bunch of idealists. Rachel doesn't come any closer than Cyprus, because she has no choice if she wants to see her fundamentalist, mentally deformed children. I go on vacation there. All the others live in Europe or the United States.'

'That wasn't the only reason,' Mony objected. 'We didn't just get together because we were Zionists. Not me. I went to escape the incredible sadness at home.'

'Me too,' I admitted.

'What exactly was it you were escaping from?' Rachel asked.

'Like you escaped your ayatollah, I escaped home,' I answered. 'My parents gave me permission to join the Zionist movement because of the educational aspects. But in fact it was the only acceptable excuse to get out and be in a safe, peaceful and relatively stable environment. It was a shelter to me.'

'Ditto,' Max said. 'But enough of this serious crap. Now I have two options. Either be a good housefather and go home or have another drink. Drive me up the hill, sonny,' he said to Michael, using a cheap phrase from the movie "The Longest Day."

'Aye aye, sir,' Michael saluted and filled Max's glass to the rim again.

'I guess we all used it as an escape,' Sally said. 'Who didn't?'

It became dead quiet.

'That's a majority,' Michael yelled victoriously. 'Resolution accepted. Long live the Queen and God bless America.'

'I needed the company,' Esther said. 'It gave me something useful and constructive to do. It was encouraging for me, talking about new challenges in the future, building a country after all the suffering and destruction in the Japanese camps and the misery after we returned to Holland.'

'I had to get away from my mother,' said Phil. 'She smothered me with her sadness. She couldn't help it, but it happened. She could not overcome the loss of her family. My family, I should say. But she had monopolized the right to mourn. Meanwhile she expected me to build a happy future she could lean on and be proud of. I couldn't carry that weight.'

'My mother also pretended to have the exclusive rights to experience pain and emotions,' Michael said. 'Emotions expressed by me and others went in one ear and out the other. If there had been an emotional antitrust law she would have been sued big. She expressed her love by taking care of an old needy lady or nursing an injured heron. But somehow we were unable to connect.'

'There was an incredible gap,' Phil said. 'Too big to comprehend. My great-grandfather was killed. That's one. My grandparents, that's two. My parents were badly injured, that's three. Esther lost her childhood in a Japanese concentration camp, that's four. We were on the run, looking for a safe shelter, that's five and God knows what we have done to our children? The fifth and sixth are better off than all the others. That's a fact. Childhood was not exactly a ball, but at least we were alive and had each other. My mother had nobody.'

'Except for you,' said Rachel.

'That's the pith of the matter,' Sally said. 'The phrase "you are all I have in life" choked me. Like there was a millstone hung around my neck. I was a replacement for all who were killed and had to make up for the losses. Thus I had to be perfect. I am not. I couldn't concentrate in school or on my homework floating in the dark stream of horror stories. I wanted to romp outside, like other kids in the street and have fun at school like my classmates.'

'Before my parents died,' said Mony, 'cruelty, depression and sadness were the only emotions at home. That's how I grew up. The ghost of Mengele was constantly present in our house.'

'So you kept that scumbag in hiding,' said Fred.

'As a matter of speech, yes,' Mony replied. 'That smothering ghost was buried along with the bodies of my parents. Only afterward, was I somewhat able to breathe.'

'We needed to know what happened during the war,' Michael said.

'Know, yes,' said Sally. 'In a coherent manner, not by overexposure of indigestible fragments. Words came down like boiling oil, burning and hurting my soul. I tried to understand but always lost track somehow. I felt like Icarus flying into the sun. As I came too close to the heat of the crematoria of the concentration camp, my wings melted. I had to have distance to protect myself. I wanted to understand, help my parents but I couldn't revive the deceased.'

'It pushed you in a corner too,' said Fred. 'Into isolation and loneliness.'

'Ultimate loneliness,' Sally responded. 'No one understood. Not the teachers in school, your classmates, the neighbors. There was no understanding aunt or uncle or any other relative. In fact we were abused. Not on purpose, but still. Even if there had been an understanding soul, I couldn't have admitted that I was abused and let my parents down. It would have been unfair, because they were honest people who loved me. They were lonely too. We had each other in a shabby clubhouse. Some of us had a brother or a sister. Our parents were left with no one to support them. And nobody really cared. Who was interested in the sad memories of a Holocaust survivor?'

It became quiet, like a few minutes of silence to commemorate the past, to pay respect to our parents and their perished beloved ones.

Max was the first to speak.

'Let's talk about the future for a minute,' he said. 'Tomorrow we devote to a brand new generation. That's the best investment we can make.'

'Don't you have to go home now?' Rachel asked.

Max sadly remained silent.

'What's wrong, Max?' Rachel asked as she put her arm around him. 'Tomorrow we celebrate David's Bar Mitzvah. There is nothing sad about that.'

'I don't have a home,' Max said as he broke out into tears. 'This is my home, not with Gaby and David. I need you so much.'

'I need you too Max,' said Esther. 'You are always there for me, I know. But we are not a family. We don't live together as some sort of cult! The day after tomorrow we return to the Diaspora and Israel. We all have to go home whether we like it or not. That's reality.'

'Maybe that's something we have in common too,' Sally said. 'Remember? At the end of each summer and winter camp, nobody wanted to go home.'

'Conclusion: We all suffer from Habonim-camp-syndrome,' said Fred. 'Darn it, you are right, we still have a difficult time going home. As children we escaped our parents. Now almost all of us have a house and family. Still there is a lack of understanding, which we do find here. We remain lonely.'

A ring of the telephone interrupted our conversation.

It was Gaby asking for Max. The family was waiting for him, including "the old bitch," his mother-in-law.

I took Max to the bathroom, cleaned his face with a wet towel, made him brush his teeth and took him down in the elevator where taxis were waiting.

'What about my car?' he asked.

'I'll bring your car tomorrow. Try to calm down on the way home. Everything is going to be fine Max.'

'It's not,' he cried. 'Damn, a couple of hours together and an entire world comes alive again. Much more than in a lifetime with my family. I wish we could stay together as a group. At least we would have each other.'

'We have each other,' I said. 'We are not alone.'

We hugged passionately, for a long time, I wiped his face again and waved goodbye as he drove off in the taxi.

'Wouldn't that be ideal?' I said to myself. 'Withdraw from reality and shelter in the safe atmosphere of the *Partners in Crime*.' Too crazy to be true.

Back in my room, Fred was sitting on my bed, playing songs on his guitar.

'It smells like a cheese factory in here,' I said.

'That must be my shoes,' Michael burped.

He got up from his chair with his shoes in his hand, opened a window and threw them out.

'I'll just wash my sweaty feet and that problem is solved.'

He went into the bathroom to wash his feet.

'Shit,' he cursed. 'Those were my only shoes. They are difficult to find because I have such big feet. Like battle ships. Only specialized stores carry my size.'

He walked back into the room to show them to us. He poured himself another large scotch, gulped it down and smiled.

'Who cares? Tomorrow is another day.'

As he said that, he collapsed on the couch and passed out, snoring loudly.

An hour later everyone left to retire except for Michael who was still in a coma on the couch, and Rachel.

'Why did you say that the only thing for sure is that nothing is for sure, earlier tonight?' Rachel asked. 'It sounds so passive, as if you don't care anymore.'

'In a sense, that's the way I feel right now.' I answered. 'I have to re-explore life. Holding on to the past leads nowhere. The future? Que sera, sera. You know, most of all, Daisy's death scared me as if I have been shadowed by death all my life. I grew up with death, fled from it. Now the first person I ever loved is dead. Like a curse. I need to get rid of that feeling.'

'But why do you say you don't you care about the future?'

I lay down on the bed. Rachel followed, putting her head on my chest.

Michael was still snoring on the couch.

'Shall we inaugurate the Sabbath by making passionate love?' I suggested. 'Your background is questionable, but you have a reasonable body for a woman your age and a good set of brains underneath your sheitel.'

'Finally you start to appreciate real beauty, intelligence and class,' Rachel responded. 'I almost can't control myself, but as a religious woman I can't let you touch me because I haven't been to the mikva for a while.'

She kissed me on the cheek.

'Now please share your thoughts with me about your future.'

'Okay,' I said. 'We all build our empires, castles or castles in the air, surrounded by high walls to hide the truth from the outside world. We have our status, power, money. We are busy, occupied; you may call it successful if you like. We are so busy that we have no time to face the truth. The truth we have shoved underneath a Persian rug. Why did Max leave us crying tonight? On the outside he has everything: A lovely wife, a healthy son, a lucrative job that he loves, a villa, money. But something is missing and terribly wrong in our foundation. Construction faults during childhood. We never take the time to build a new solid foundation so we can safely build our lives on it. Ours is too fragile. We don't build a solid new foundation because we are too busy with our careers. We punished ourselves with high mortgages for houses that are too expensive. Fred talked about being pushed into the corner of loneliness tonight. Do we have to carry on that way? We unsuccessfully have tried to come to terms with the past, to mourn for relatives we never met. When Daisy died, mourning became realistic to me. Daisy was for real. We touched, laughed, cried, argued, made love. We lived. Her death was realistic. Tangibly realistic! It's up to me to use this tragedy as a stepping stone to a better quality of the second part of my life. I owe her that, I owe it to myself. Call it a moment of reorientation. I voluntarily take distance from the tax deductible castles in the air and my artificial status. Painful? Not really. Necessary. Nothing has a real meaning if you don't create happiness and stability that you can share with others. People are conservative, afraid of change. Well, I have no choice, so now I grab the opportunity and finally take my time. People may think that I have lost it, that I am lazy. They are uncomfortable with my present lifestyle because it lacks security and everyone likes to be in control. What a waste of talent, they say. Of what? I'm not hurting anyone. I thought that I was always in control until Daisy crashed. So in fact I wasn't. Put that in your pipe and smoke it. Now I am not scared anymore that life cannot be controlled sometimes, that there are more powerful elements. I just try to rearrange my life. Maybe in a year or two I'll happily look back over my shoulder, looking at a new, peaceful past that I like. One that I have created myself, leaving the shadow of death behind me. Death will then be ahead of me. One day we all die. Until that moment we need to live, not to survive.'

'You are not as stupid as I thought,' Rachel smiled. 'I think you made the right decision, but it's going to be a long and bumpy, lonely road.'

'That doesn't frighten me. On the contrary. Perhaps I will be able to get rid of the melody and lyrics of "The March of the Deceased" that still haunts my brain.* I have to erase that from my memory. That's the way I want to carry on.'

'May I be a witness for a long time to come,' Rachel whispered as she hugged me.

In that position we fell asleep and woke up the next morning, in each other's arms with our clothes on. Michael was still snoring on the couch.

* See page 6 and 7 of this book.

14

The Saturday morning Sabbath service started in style. Each chair was occupied and most of the people had given much attention to their outfits. They had come to see and be seen. Max and his family were nervous and emotional.

I immediately understood why Max called his mother-in-law "an old bitch." Even before the service started she tried to control the cause of events, whispering "instructions" too loudly, trying to give irritating, dramatic signed signals to David in an attempt to manipulate him into what to do and how to act. She unhappily failed as a director. David took it like a young hero and managed to keep his act together.

My *Partners in Crime* looked surprisingly well, considering the lack of sleep and overconsumption of alcoholic beverages the night before. Everyone had taken sufficient time to revive, dress up appropriately and arrive at the synagogue early enough to greet David, Max, Gaby and "the old bitch." Only Michael was missing. He was nowhere to be found. His timing was perfect. Well into the service, just when David started his first bracha, a sweaty and out of breath Michael came running loudly down the aisle. He was dressed in a black tie, his pants tucked into bright, yellow, rubber fisherman's boots. He looked like a clown. People tried to control themselves but couldn't.

It became painfully quiet for a moment. Then there was a burst of laughter, including the rabbi who had tears in his eyes, leaning on David's shoulder.

'I apologize,' Michael said after it became quiet again. 'I lost my shoes last night. In this neighborhood there is no store that carries my size.'

Everybody hee-hawed and applauded.

'I can't help it,' he continued. 'I tried everywhere. I spent over an hour in a taxi, in my socks until I found these boots in an angling store.'

He pulled up one leg so everyone could see his jackboots.

After another big laugh the rabbi thanked him politely for his kind explanation, the complementary entertainment and the sharing of his interpretation of the laws of the Sabbath. Everyone, including David was more relaxed after this little incident, except for "the old bitch" who called Michael a schmuck.

Following the service there was a crowded reception with coffee and cake. Rachel took me by the arm which I appreciated as I had not been to a big social function since Daisy's death. She provided me with a loving sense of security.

'How do you like me as your escort this afternoon?' she asked.

'Just for the afternoon?'

'Maybe much longer. That depends on you.'

'Wouldn't that be an easy way out?' I said. 'An easy emotional shortcut. After the dramatic death of his wife he returned to the perfect match, the woman that he should have married to begin with. The gorgeous, religious princess, under who's short, sexy skirt waited a new paradise of desire, love and lust. They made passionate love, got married and lived long and unhappily for rest of their lives.'

'I didn't hear the end of your sentence,' Rachel responded, purposely pushing her warm breast into my arm. 'Can't you just let go?'

'I already did,' I answered. 'I admit that it was a delight waking up in your arms and I don't deny that some old feelings, that I had presumed dead, seem to have revived. You are cute too.'

I kissed her on the cheek.

'Welcome back to the real world,' Rachel responded. 'I love you too.'

After the reception we picked up the present we had ordered for David. We had discussed this at length during a conference call amongst *The Partners in Crime* before we left for New York. We gave our Bar Mitzvah present to David, that night, at his dinner party.

'When we were your age we were given our father's old watch on our Bar Mitzvah,' I said to David in what supposed to be a brief speech. 'When I got mine I felt proud and happy, until I discovered that this was the only opportunity for my dad, the nebech, to buy a brand new watch for himself, without being guilt-tripped by my mother that he was egoistically wasting too much money on unnecessary gadgets. Of course I need to mention that our Yiddishe mama spent more on hairdressers than NASA does on its entire space program. A Yiddishe mama has the undisputed privilege to be unreasonable and irrational. She always claims to be on a rigid diet but eats homemade chocolate cake every afternoon. If, in her opinion you do something wrong, which is often, she will forgive you after a brief dramatic argument but she won't forget and will keep hinting at it until judgment day.

She also has the self-proclaimed right to explode over nothing, hysterically collapse and whine for hours in Yiddish and Polish, so you don't understand but are forced to listen. The average Yiddishe papa is her subordinate, the prototype of a schlemiel. In society and at work he is an honorable personality whose opinion is highly respected. At home he is the shlemazel who gets blamed for all that goes wrong and he thinks twice before talking back, if at all. That's why my dad, the bungler, needed his son's Bar Mitzvah as a legitimate excuse to buy himself a new fifty dollar watch. Fortunately a watch is no longer a luxury item, so you probably got one when you were six or seven. It used to be tradition to be passing on a legacy like a chanukiah or a kiddush cup on a Bar Mitzvah. If you were lucky you got this from a family member who was still alive and could give it to you himself. As old *Partners in Crime* we would have loved to give you such a treasure that we inherited.'

'Write him a check,' Fred yelled. 'That's not a real present but at least a compensation for your shtuss.'

'Shut up Fred,' I said. 'Give me a chance to concentrate.'

'On what?' Leslie asked. 'Are you retarded? Just say a few words and give that child his present. A ten year old can do that.'

'We wanted to give you something that is not for sale in stores,' I continued.

'That's cheap,' Joan interrupted. 'Why pass him a white elephant? Don't you feel embarrassed at all? Shame on you.'

'It is indeed embarrassing that we almost stood here empty handed,' I continued. 'The few precious items that survived the war became statues for the deceased. We didn't want to pass that on to you. That's why we were empty handed.'

'So get lost and pass the microphone to someone who isn't,' Michael yelled, obviously enjoying the excellent wine. 'Or maybe Fred can sing one of his prehistoric songs.'

'The only solution was, to start over again, have it newly made. So recreating an old tradition we give you this silver kiddush-cup with our names engraved. For you to use in good health for a long time every Sabbath. And hopefully to pass on one day to your children or another relative. I sincerely hope that one day you will say, I got this from a bunch of substitute aunts and uncles, now I am passing it on to you, recreating our old tradition.'

As I said this, Max's mother-in-law burst into tears. David understood the message, I could tell. It was good to see, but a few seconds later I realized that we had just infected yet another generation with the virus of death and cruelty.

I didn't have much time for thoughts.

'Would you be available tomorrow morning?' Aunt Suzy asked me, as I was heading back to my seat.

'Are you trying to shadchen me again Suzele?'

She nodded with a big smile.

'As long as I am around I am telling you that a man like you should not be alone too long. I know you and I know what is good for you. You need a sweet, caring wife. Now, tomorrow this nice young lady is coming to visit me. She is the daughter of...'

I kissed Aunt Suzy on the cheek.

'You still act as if you are on commission,' I whispered in her ear.

The "China man" next to her laughed and twinkled at me.

In fact Aunt Suzy was nobody's aunt. She had been Gaby's piano teacher since early childhood and had become "part of the inventory," as she used to call it. Now, in her late eighties, she was still energetic and always in a good mood, even though health problems forced her to leave her condominium and live in a nursing home. It looked more like a luxurious hotel or country club than a home for the elderly. Excellent meals were served to her suite, overlooking a golf course.

Nevertheless, when somebody asked her how she was doing she answered: 'Not bad, considering they put me in this mental institution.' The word "they" sounded as if her family had made her move, but she had no family and always made her own decisions.

Suzy was born in Berlin. She was the only daughter in a very religious Jewish family of ten children. She fell in love with Ingo, a gentile who was in medical school. When she announced she was going to marry him, the family cut her off because her husband-to-be was not Jewish. The men ripped their clothes as if someone had died and in fact they had a shiva for her. To her parents, brothers and sisters, she was dead. The rest of the family ignored her too after she married Ingo.

In 1938 she tried to re-establish contact with her family. As she approached the home where she grew up she witnessed Nazis looting the house and her father's bookstore. The entire inventory was set on fire. Her father and one of her brothers were dragged out onto the street, their payess and beards were cut, they were kicked and humiliated. Her father and oldest brother were thrown into an army truck and taken away.

The next morning Suzy went back to the house. The broken windows were boarded-up, walls covered with soot and ashes. She peeked in through a chink. She vaguely saw the faces of two of her little brothers and her mother.

Suzy begged them to let her in.

'We can help you,' she desperately yelled at the locked door. 'For goodness' sake, come with me or they are going to kill you all.'

There was no response. In their minds Suzy was dead.

Her husband Ingo tried to establish contact twice. The first time they wouldn't let him in, the second time the house was empty. They had all been deported to Dachau.

Ingo was a member of a small resistance cell at the university. Mostly young intellectuals of well-to-do families. They had reliable sources and knew from the beginning that Hitler was a psychopath, a killing dictator who would destroy Germany in a bloody manner. They provided Suzy with a new, non-Jewish identity, including a forged passport. They lived as an ordinary German couple in a comfortable apartment.

In 1942, after he finished his studies, Ingo was drafted. He decided to fulfill his duties, only to be a safe cover for Suzy, who became the well respected spouse of a Wehrmacht officer. He was appointed to run a field hospital. He even got decorated with the Iron Cross for bravery after he got slightly wounded. He showed the medal to Suzy when he was on a short leave in 1943.

'If I get killed, I want you to send it to Der Führer in a blank envelope with a note, wishing him a lengthy, painful, terminal disease,' he instructed Suzy.

Fortunately he survived.

Suzy languished in feelings of guilt, having been unable to rescue any one of her family.

'It's bizarre,' she said. 'In their eyes I was the one who sinned and was declared dead. In reality I was the only one to survive. Very harrowing. I keep asking myself if I could have done more, especially for my youngest brother. He was blond with blue eyes, just like me. Ingo could have provided him with a new identity. He could have stayed with us. Nobody would have noticed anything unusual. It kept me awake for many nights. Just before they were deported I walked to the corner of the street of my parental home. He was riding his tricycle on the sidewalk. My mother saw me and grabbed him into the house before I could make a move.'

In late 1943 Ingo deserted the army. He had worked out a plan to escape to Switzerland. The Swiss borders had been hermetically closed, but doors could be opened silently in exchange for a substantial amount of cash or valuables. Ingo's deceased father had been an art collector. With a little luck and a lot of knowledge he had build a collection beyond valuation. He was owner of a Rembrandt, several pieces of Jan Steen, Rubens and Renoirs.

Ingo's aged mother insisted in using the collection for Ingo and Suzy to escape from Germany.

'I am an old woman,' she said. 'I'll be fine. Your father secured good financial arrangements for me before he passed away. What do I do with a bunch of paintings if my son gets killed in a ridiculous war that won't stop before Hitler has killed all Jews and Germany will be in ruins. You and Suzy may have a wonderful future ahead of you. Please, take that opportunity.'

Without major complications Ingo and Suzy succeeded in crossing the Swiss border. Ingo's father had stored his collection with a friend in Geneva, Switzerland in 1934 when it became clear to him that Germany was heading for disaster. That friend sold the collection, bribed authorities on both sides of the border and made sure that there were sufficient funds for Ingo and Suzy to set up a new life in Geneva.

Ingo got a good job as a doctor at a local hospital, Suzy worked as a teacher and meanwhile studied for her degree at the Academy of Music. Ingo's mother was killed in the last days of the war during one of the allied bombardments of Berlin.

In 1948 Ingo was offered a teaching position at UCLA. Once settled in Los Angeles Suzy gave piano lessons. Ingo continued his studies and became a highly sought after neurologist. In 1954 he was appointed professor at a University hospital in New York where they bought a big penthouse. In 1962 Ingo suddenly died of a massive heart attack and left Suzy wealthy, but inconsolable.

Not until her late seventies did she see another man, the "China man," as she called him. He was not at all Chinese, but a German Jew.

Alfred was also born in Berlin. In 1939 the Nazis allowed him to leave the country in exchange for the entire estate of his parents. His belongings were carefully loaded into a truck to be transported to the vessel that would take Alfred to South America. The goods never arrived. Stolen by the Nazis. After many delays and badgering, Alfred arrived in Hamburg. By that time all escape routes were cut off, except for Shanghai, China.

In 1946 a surviving friend of his perished parents sent him a boat ticket to New York. He took two jobs and worked day and night to finance his law studies. He married and had two children.

He and his wife divorced after the youngest child went off to college. Alfred devoted all of his time to his law practice and did not socialize much until a friend invited him to a charity concert, to raise money for a hospital in Israel. That's where he met Suzy.

Suzy and Alfred started dating. Whenever one was invited to a social gathering, the other came along. They went to concerts, movies, museums and several times on a cruise.

'I am dating a "China man," Suzy always said.

He referred to her as "The Tramp" because she moved so many times.

'You better stay away from that tramp,' Alfred warned me. 'The moment she smells a single person the old demented, fossil bolts completely. It brings out the worst in her. I guess she was born that way.' He got up, took me by the arm and guided me to a little espresso bar in a quiet corner.

'Tell your friends that I salute them for the appropriate and elegant gesture you made to David,' he said. 'I myself tried so many times to express what you said to him, on behalf of your pals. How come they listen to you and not to me?'

'Elaborate,' I responded.

'It's strange,' he explained. 'I was a lucky man. My parents spent all of their assets in 1939 to help me escape from Germany, just in time. Soon they were both arrested. These criminals stripped them. After that, they were of no further use so they were disposed of. My stay in Shanghai was not exactly a luxurious vacation, but ever since I came to The States, I got every opportunity in the world. I am proud of my children and grandchildren. Bless God I am healthy, but no one was ever really interested in my past. I tried to talk about it to my ex-wife, but she told me to stop because it kept her awake at night. Our kids are born and raised in America. They went to good colleges and universities, but they hardly learned anything about the Holocaust, let alone my background. For thirty years I worked with a woman. First she was my secretary, later my assistant and finally my business partner. A remarkable young lady. Intelligent, interested in mostly everything, open minded, honest. I supported her studies. She is fluent in five languages. Once she came across a magazine article on my desk, written by a friend of mine. She read it and then asked me what the Crystal Night was. I couldn't believe it after all of her studies. Shortly afterwards she asked me about Mengele. As I started to tell her she interrupted me. She could not stand the cruelty. It made me feel isolated. Even intelligent, decent people, friends with a good background and education, don't know or don't want to know. Sometimes I feel like I have been contaminated with an infectious disease, just because I am a so-called "survivor" whose family was killed under the most disgusting circumstances. My past is a disease. I am being punished for a crime against my family and friends. Or maybe it's apathy. That's even worse. A friend of mine who used to work for the Mossad once told me that more than likely they could have caught Mengele.

The house of his wife in the Italian part of Tyrol was monitored. Just prior to Mengele's birthday, she made preparations for a trip with a lot of luggage. The Israeli agents observing the house, reported her departure and suggested that she should be followed, the house searched and bugged. The agents were called off the job. Just to quit. Left wing elements within the organization didn't want Menachem Begin to score another success after the peace treaty with Egypt. The Brussels stationed commander literally said that, "Catching Mengele would provide Begin with another two Knesset seats." Politics before justice, but what else is new? Years later it appeared to be questionable that Mengele was still alive at that time but no one knew that back then. For a while I believed that perhaps people had learned a lesson from the Holocaust, but that's not true. They witness one genocide and bloody war after the other on TV and watch it with dry eyes. Maybe you think now that I am telling you more than you wanted to know, you have your own tsoris too. I don't know. However, when I heard you talk to David tonight you gave me the feeling that there are people who understand and care. At least that means that I am not completely alone in that respect. Now, enough lectures from an old retarded "China man." Let's go eat.'

Alfred returned to his seat next to Suzy. She hand-signaled me, to try and resume her efforts as a matchmaker but I stuck my tongue out to her and she gave me one of her great, beautiful smiles in return.

15

Fred played his guitar. He had written a few new songs for the occasion. Funny songs, describing all of the anxiety that a family creates while planning an extremely expensive Bar Mitzvah party that is supposed to be picture perfect.

'Why should we invite Gideon? He always gets into arguments with the entire family.'

'So why invite your brother Nate? The day after your father passed away he went on a vacation to London. He didn't even attend the shiva. Besides, he'll get into a fight again with his ex-wife and their children will refuse to sit at the same table with him.'

Fred also touched all of the snobbish issues related to the astronomical amounts spent on these kind of parties, just to show that the family is well to do. Fred's jokes hit the spot. David and his family were laughing constantly, except for "the old bitch" who called him a nudnick.

Fred's jokes were all too familiar to me. My parents had not talked to my brother Eric since the day that he had asked my father for a small loan to buy a wedding suit.

When Daisy and I were going to get married we felt like we were caught between a rock and a hard place. We wanted to invite just a small group of beloved ones and keep it simple. It would have been virtually impossible to invite both my parents and my brother and his family. At the same token it would have been unheard of to invite only one party of the same tribe. Each solution would lead to unpleasant arguments.

In an attempt to resolve this problem, I innocently and with open eyes stepped into quicksand.

'Maybe this is the appropriate occasion to organize a peace summit,' I suggested to Daisy.

Daisy didn't answer. Just gave me a despairing look.

'Perhaps Eric's children will get to see their grandparents. Wouldn't that be nice?' I defined my plan.

'You do whatever your heart tells you to do,' Daisy reacted. 'You know I will always support you. But please, also make a plan B, because I intend to get married only once in my life and preferably not in a minefield.'

That sounded reasonable.

I suggested to my brother and my parents to meet with good intentions, a week prior to the wedding. This would give me some leeway if plan B needed to be implemented. In case my diplomatic efforts would be regrettably insufficient. My brother wanted me to act as a mediator, which I refused. Why did adults need a referee?

My father wanted to know what would happen if the reconciliation attempt wouldn't work out.

'I'm not flying all the way from Amsterdam to New York to discover that my son is still stubborn and impossible,' he threatened.

'Why so negative?' I asked. 'It shouldn't be so difficult to just say: "Hi, good to see you" and let go of the past. Take it from there.'

Eric persisted in me being the mediator.

'How can I make an appointment with someone who refuses to communicate?'

I knew that my shuttle diplomacy was about to explode into my face, but didn't want to hear about a way back. I was sucked into the quicksand up to my knees by now.

'All right,' I gave in. 'I will arrange for the meeting.' To show that I was no weakling, I added, 'I will set the date and place, but from then on you're on your own.'

Daisy kept silent, but the expression on her face confirmed my deepest fears.

A week prior to the wedding I went to the Plaza Hotel in New York where I had reserved a small meeting room. Not the ideal setting. A couple of tables, chairs, soft drinks and a thermos with coffee. There were no alternatives though.

Daisy insisted that the meeting should not be held at our home, but on neutral territory.

'If it goes wrong I'm stuck with two angry parents, just before my marriage. I don't want to discourage you, but we should draw a line here, just in case.'

Eric's wife was slightly more outspoken.

'I'll have them arrested for trespassing, the moment they enter my property,' she threatened. 'I personally could not care less if I ever see them again.'

A bar or restaurant were out of the question, because my father would get into an embarrassing exchange of words with a waiter. It was too cold to sit down for any length of time on a bench in Central Park. A meeting room in a hotel remained the only solution.

My diplomatic mission was exhausting and looked more complicated to me than the Middle East peace process. However, within the margins little progress was made, such as a laborious compromise on the protocol! But my father didn't want to see Eric before he had apologized to him.

Eric found it unacceptable that my father had attached a precondition to a meeting with "an open agenda" before it even started. I energetically spent over an hour negotiating on two phones relaying their respective messages and demands. I felt the quicksand sucking me in rapidly, especially since Daisy behaved as if she were watching a soap opera. Each time I attempted to settle another segment of my phone conversation with diplomacy, she poured herself a glass of wine, lit a cigarette, comfortably leaned back in her chair and enjoyed. To make things worse she started to call me "Mister Ambassador" and twice she sung John Lennon's "Give Peace a Chance" in the shower, later she switched to Paul Simon's "You've got to learn how to fall before you learn to fly."

I acted as if I didn't care. With a lot of determination and perseverance I enforced a final agreement on the protocol. Eric would arrive at noon, my parents fifteen minutes later! I would separately escort them to the meeting room. Then they would take it from there, while I would wait outside.

Eric and his wife arrived on the dot. I brought them a Mad Magazine to kill the time before my parents arrived.

I walked Eric into the meeting room, Irene obstinately, settled in the lounge.

'What are you going to do if they get into an argument and walk out of there?' she arrogantly asked me.

'Oh well, don't doom the day before it's over,' I answered, but these words did not convince her nor me. For once we agreed.

Fortunately our conversation was short because my parents arrived early. They ignored Irene who grumpily stared at her shoes. My father took a seat ten feet down the hall, facing the other way. He assigned my mother as messenger, still refusing to meet Eric before he apologized to him.

After thirty seconds she returned from the meeting room.

'He is not ready to apologize,' she reported to my father.

'I told you so,' my father answered as he got up to walk out.

My mother nervously stopped him.

'Please don't rush things now,' she said. 'Let me talk to him again.'

Now it took almost a minute for her to return.

'Eric wants to know what it is that you want him to apologize for?' she timidly asked my father.

Apparently he had not anticipated this question that obviously took him by surprise. Clearly aggravated it took him a few seconds to formulate an answer.

'For misbehavior and insulting his parents,' was the charge.

My mother had another brief conversation with Eric and came back with the question if my father could be more specific.

It confused my father. He tried to formulate a more specific accusation but he might have had too long a list of reproaches to rapidly make up his mind.

'You don't even know what you are blaming him for?' Irene snapped at him. 'That's why you threw him out of his house?'

'That does it,' my father reacted and angrily walked away, followed by my mother who tried to calm him down.

'You may come out of the closet,' I told Eric. 'It was a priceless farce. Those melodrama's are only to be found on Broadway. Two adults being angry and stubborn only separated by a wall, refusing to talk.'

'I told you it wouldn't work,' Irene commented.

They went home and left me in the hotel with my parents. As I was standing in the elevator, on my way to their room, I was hastily thinking of creative solutions. My emergency plan was cowardly but effective. We could fly to the West Coast, get married and go on a honeymoon to a luxurious resort, far away from arguing family. But I found that rude to my parents who had come all the way from Europe. Feeling insecure I knocked on their door. Fortunately the problem solved itself. When I walked into their room my mother was packing their suitcases. My father had locked himself into the bathroom with a book.

'He doesn't want to stay one minute longer,' my mother said. 'Maybe it's for the best. I'm not going to argue with him. If we stay, he would ruin your party. Here, give this to Daisy for me.' She gave me Daisy's wedding present, wrapped in paper that had been used on countless previous festive occasions.

'Shall I wait until he comes out of the bathroom?' I asked.

'You'd better not, he won't come out until you are gone. He is mad at Eric, at me, at you. You know him when he becomes impossible. He stops communicating.'

'That is communicating too,' I said before I left.

After I told the whole drama to Daisy she asked, 'Can you recall any family party or gathering that did not end in arguments and anxiety?'

I didn't answer her question. No, I was unable to recall one happy, relaxed family gathering. Days prior to my sixth birthday I decided to never ever celebrate my birthday again, because parties always resulted in arguments and yelling. Children's parties didn't fit the circumstances.

I remembered my parents fighting behind the closed kitchen door.

'Why did we invite a bunch of whining, noisy, bad mannered children? We have our hands full with our own impossible kids.'

Daisy unwrapped my mother's wedding gift. A big, previously

owned glossy book: "*Pictures of The Holocaust.*"

'Let's go out to dinner and forget what happened today,' Daisy suggested.

During a romantic dinner we cheered up and started to make new wedding plans.

'Either we play it by the rules, or we don't,' she said. 'Why be gracious to a sanctimonious rabbi who even refuses to shake hands with a woman after a hysterectomy at age seventy?' she stated. 'Nor do I wish to associate with one of these cults where there are gentile, female rabbi's wearing yarmulkes. It throws me off.

Self-proclaimed Jews who go blank if you use a Yiddish expression and don't know how to prepare gefilte fish or kreplach. I'd rather treat a judge to a little cheer in between arguing power-tie layers.'

'We could get married in Israel,' I suggested. 'Quickly fly up and down and give a small dinner party after we return.'

'No way,' Daisy responded determinedly. 'Rabbi's demand tips there and I don't want an orthodox wedding. Wedding ceremonies in Israel are usually tasteless. Remember these parties? The average bride looks like a contestant on "The Love Connection," the guests even tackier, wearing the most hideous outfits imaginable. The bride's dress, that makes people dizzy, is made out of enough material to clothe the population of China, expressing the concept "my designer created a perfectly beautiful, simple dress, and then kept adding on to it until it required a building permit." No one pays attention to the religious ceremony. It's just considered as a short break between hors d'oeuvres and the main course. They invite over a thousand guests who dance to loud disco music and afterwards leave a check behind, covering the expenses of the caterer. The female guests wear skirts or dresses that are too short to cover their private parts and at least two sizes too small, they wear enough cosmetics to make it look like Andy Warhol put it on, at least one bra strap needs to be shown and they wear more gold and diamonds than the entire collection of Tiffany's. Instead of dancing in a circle with disco music I have something better in mind. Let's go to court and spend our money on the honeymoon.'

We made arrangements for a delightful honeymoon. We planned to return to the place where we first met, the Mark Hopkins hotel in San Francisco.

At the Court House we paid a small fee to the clerk. We took a seat on the public stand of a courtroom, observing arguments and disputes on divorces and fighting neighbors; small crimes. After half an hour the judge appeared to have some spare time and ordered us to step forward to him. As if in a side bar conference, he rapidly asked us the necessary questions. After we made the promise "for better and for worse" he slammed his hammer on his bench. Everybody stood up. Angry couples, suspects and attorneys applauded loudly. This was tolerated for thirty seconds after which another loud bang with the hammer indicated that the judge wanted to return to the order of the day and that Daisy and I were united in matrimony. Next case.

After this "ceremony" Dave had arranged for lunch at the Top of the Mark. He had reserved a table with a view of the roof of Dick and Beverly's roof terrace. They had been invited too. Awaiting their arrival, Daisy had gone to our room to freshen up.

'What happened to your bride?' Beverly asked.

'She went off to make a quickie with the bell captain,' said Dave. 'The safest time to cheat on your spouse is during the honeymoon, because no one in his right mind expects you to do it.'

'Thank you for bringing it up again,' Leslie reacted, slapping him on the arm.

On the first day of their honeymoon Dave had been flirting with a pretty, young lady at the pool side while Leslie took an afternoon nap. The lady took Dave to her room and treated him to oral sex. Unfortunately for Dave, she became a little too excited and bit him. Not real hard but enough to leave some bloody teeth marks that hurt severely. Not only did he suffer visual damage, but each time he got an erection he was in severe pain, preventing them from having intercourse; one of the possible joys of a romantic honeymoon. When Leslie noticed his injuries, he told her that while shaving he had hurt himself leaning on the wall in the bathroom and got stuck in the bottle opener.

Of course, Leslie didn't believe a word of what he told her.

'I was ready to chop it off all together,' Leslie said. 'But I didn't, out of self-interest.'

'I would have done it,' Beverly said. 'I would have put it in the kitchen grinder, made pâté out of it and served it to him on his sick bed.'

'Can we talk about something else on my honeymoon?' I asked.

A tray with snacks was served but the pâté remained untouched. Only Dave took some.

'Tastes good,' he informed us. 'Especially since I know how they prepare these things.'

Daisy came in, wearing the same outfit as the day we had met; a sexy, short black evening dress.

After lunch we went downstairs to the lounge. Dick had hired the same piano player we had enjoyed the night Daisy and I had been coupled by Beverly. We listened and talked for several hours after which we walked to Dick and Beverly's penthouse.

On the roof terrace stood a bottle of champagne in a cooler and two glasses. Dick and Beverly went down to their penthouse. Daisy and I were left together on the same spot, in the same position as that first night. My head comfortably resting on her warm shoulder. I gave her a necklace made out of golden daisies and a matching bracelet. She never took them off again.

'Why is this night different from other nights, especially the night we met?' I asked her in Passover style.

'Tomorrow we will stay together, I don't have to let you go like the first time,' she answered. 'I'm never going to let go of you. We are inseparable.'

'Is that a promise or a threat?' I asked.

'A blessing,' she answered.

The next morning we drove down Pacific Coast Highway into the direction of Los Angeles. We enjoyed three gorgeous days, driving along the coastline, staying a couple of nights at a beach front hotel, watching the seals and seagulls, walking the beach and having little picnics on the rocks.

Pierre had invited us and a couple of friends for a luncheon at Café Montmartre. His wife Simone was there, Daisy's sister and brother-in-law.

Daisy proudly showed her new jewels to her sister.

'No diamonds?' she reproached me. 'Didn't you even give her a nice gem for her wedding? Well, perhaps you are just stingy, as all Dutch are.'

Her husband felt a developing tension and tried to change the subject. He started to tell Pierre about a new Mercedes he had bought.

'In Europe we use them as taxis,' Pierre teased him. 'Because diesel is cheap. Illegal construction recruiters pick up wetbacks with these cars. And they are used by pimps and boasters with advertisement

agencies who think it's a status symbol. No one in his right mind would want to drive around in a Nazi car with that logo on the hood.'
'Why not?' my brand new brother-in-law asked.
'You are not bothered by too much knowledge,' Pierre responded.
He turned around and told us the latest jokes he had heard from Paris.

Daisy and I drove to Long Beach to take a helicopter to Catalina Island. A romantic oasis of silence and paradise-like nature. When we arrived, we asked someone to take a picture with my camera. Daisy and I in front of a helicopter at the heliport of Avalon. She would always carry that picture with her, wherever she went.

We spent an unforgettable week there, enjoying ourselves like little children, driving the picturesque winding mountain roads with a golf cart. After each curve there was another breathtaking view. We spent days on a small motorboat, mainly floating around, watching large schools of colored fish and corals underneath us. Seals and seagulls surrounded us when we threw out leftover food. Dolphins danced around the boat. Each morning we had breakfast on the patio of our hotel room, overlooking the harbor, where people were maneuvering their boats. It was the most precious and harmonious trip thinkable, overwhelmed by love.
We decided to return there every year to celebrate our anniversary. We religiously stuck to that happy commitment. Whether we lived in Connecticut or Holland, we always returned to that pretty island, happier each year. Until death did us part.

My parents could not get over my brother's alleged intolerable behavior. My father phoned me in Catalina in an attempt try to get rid of his anger. I got upset and asked him if he had lost his mind, disturbing our peaceful honeymoon.

He was slightly amused by my anger.

'Now you talk exactly like your uncle Nathan did,' he laughed. 'He was short fused like you. Actually, you resemble him a lot, only he was much more intelligent.'

I was a clone copy of one of his perished brothers, only of lesser quality? An interesting thought.

16

After Fred's successful performance at the Bar Mitzvah dinner, David came to see me. He thanked me again for the present and asked: 'Are you getting together tonight, after the party? Like yesterday?'

'I think so,' I answered him. 'We haven't talked about it, but I'm sure no one will go directly to their room after your party.'

'My dad says it was lots of fun yesterday. Can I come too, tonight?'

'Yes, if your parents have no objections, why not?' I answered.

Together we walked to Max and Gaby.

'You can only celebrate your Bar Mitzvah once,' Gaby responded. 'If this is your big wish. It's your day so do whatever you want. I am only concerned about your dad. When he made an emergency landing in bed last night, he smelled like an Irish pub at closing time. I needed a canon to wake him up his morning. He had the worst hangover ever. I had to shlep him into the shower.'

A little after ten o'clock the dinner party was over. We said goodbye to Max and Gaby's family and went up to my room to finish the leftovers goodies from the night before and to chat some more. Only Max was absent. He didn't want to leave Gaby alone again with a house full of guests and relatives.

In the elevator David asked me: 'Is it true what they say, that you won't go home anymore?'

'I don't know yet,' I answered him. 'It's almost been a year since I've been there.'

'Don't you miss your home?'

'A little bit,' I said. 'I try not to think about it too much.'

'Do you think you'll miss Daisy if you go home?' he asked.

'Well, missing is not the right word, David. You know, it's strange, you are the first one to ask direct questions on that subject that I can answer.'

'Am I not supposed to do that?'

'On the contrary. It's good. You get right to the point. I'll try to explain to you exactly why I find it hard to go home. I kept running into myself. When I came home late I routinely, quietly closed the front door and was sneaking into the house until I realized that there was no one anymore to reckon with. I didn't need to be quiet, I wasn't disturbing anyone. On my way home, on Friday afternoons I automatically stopped at the florist to buy Daisy a nice bouquet for Sabbath. But once inside I realized, "I don't need to do this anymore." Throughout the years there were hundreds, maybe thousands of habits that became routine. They constantly reminded me of the harsh reality that life had changed forever. Each time, that hurts beyond description. It simply takes a long time for that grief to wear away, I guess. Does that make sense to you or am I talking balderdash?'

'No, I totally understand,' David answered. 'We used to have a dog at home, as long as I could recall. Two months ago the vet had to put him to sleep because he was irreversibly sick and in pain. My mom and I decided that he didn't deserve that, so we took him to the vet for a final visit. We had to. He had a beautiful life. I didn't feel guilty about it, but when I came home from school I expected him to greet me, to jump and to wag his tail with his lead in his mouth, because he knew that I would take him for a walk. But there were no more walks. Before dinner I automatically went to the kitchen to feed him, but that was no longer necessary. Each morning as I woke up I stepped out of bed very carefully, because I knew he used to sleep there. Every time that happened and I discovered that he was no longer there, I had to swallow. I still do, but it is gradually becoming less.'

'That's exactly as it is,' I said. 'Each time you have to swallow. I don't want to do that to myself, so I don't really want to go home for a while.'

'What is a while?' David asked.

'I don't know, as long as it takes. Maybe I'll create another home, somewhere else. When you are troubled it sometimes is difficult to look into the future. Usually your vision is three dimensional, so you have perspective. Past, present, future. You are able to look forward to the events of tomorrow and beyond, maybe a year along the road. Right now I am unable to do that. Everything looks flat and colorless. So, I live by the day until it gets better. I know it will, but I don't know when that will be. Meanwhile I just have to carry on.'

David appeared to digest my words with a serious look. As we entered my room, my *Partners in Crime* had made themselves at home. Some other guests had joined the party that appeared to be cheerful. David stayed close to me. Suddenly he said, 'I feel exactly the way you do when you describe the future. Sometimes it's beautiful and looks three dimensional. Right now it's all flat and I don't like it a bit. Only bad things will happen. I feel like I've had it.'

Mony had listened to the conversation.

'Why do you say that?' he asked David. 'What is it you don't like?'

'I don't like anything,' he answered, almost in tears. 'It's like everything is going wrong.'

'Where? At home, in school? Today everything went fine,' Mony said. 'What's wrong?'

'Everything,' David answered. 'I don't get anything done properly, nothing is going my way. I feel worthless.'

'What do you mean?' Mony insisted.

'Everything is going wrong,' David repeated. 'For this stupid Bar Mitzvah that my grandmother wanted, I had to attend special classes. That was all I needed, another class. I have my piano lessons and have to practice an hour every day. I get plenty of homework so I don't have time playing ball outside with my friends. I can't even use the excuse anymore that I have to walk the dog. Sometimes I lie to my mom that I don't have any homework and go play outside. Then I screw up at school.'

'Does that happen often?' Mony asked.

'Too many times. Shortly the bubble will burst when I get my school report. I don't think my parents will be pleased and when they get upset I get grounded, so I cannot play outside and meet with my friends at all. I think that I'm in deep trouble.'

'I don't think so,' Mony said. 'You're almost in big trouble. They are still avoidable.'

'You tell me how?' David asked cynically.

'Listen,' Mony said. 'In fact you're doing fine. You learn a lot. All these lessons make sense. It doesn't come easy, brother. It all takes time. Nobody can expect a man your age to manage time well enough so that you can accomplish everything and still find sufficient time to relax. There are adults with a university degree in Time Management who frequently screw up. You must go to school, do your homework, practice the piano, follow your lessons in Judaism. That can be expected. But managing your time so you can play and relax too is something that cannot be expected from someone your age. If you want me to, I'll talk to your dad. If he only had known he would have helped you already, I'm sure. It needs to be discussed at home and at school. They'll understand and give you a fair chance. School kids are busy. Everybody knows that.'

'That sounds good,' David said. 'Would you do that for me? Talk to my dad?'

'You got it,' Mony promised. 'Problems are there to be solved. Not to drag on. In other words, I'll go to my room now to phone your dad. You go and have fun with the others. If you keep that grumpy look on your face you'll look even worse than your father did this morning.'

Mony went to his room to call Max who listened quietly before he responded.

'It's a thrill a minute,' he said. 'Never a dull moment. I'm kidding. I'm glad you guys talked. Gaby knew that something wasn't kosher for a while, but he wouldn't talk to her. We will straighten it all out with David. It happened. No crying over spilled milk. It's my mistake too, it happened in my house. Tell David not to worry anymore as of the day of his Bar Mitzvah. We'll help him out, that's only fair.'

When Mony walked back into my room he briefed David on the conversation with Max.

'Now it's up to you and your parents to constructively work on the future. Don't waste your time on depressive thoughts. That's no longer necessary. Just accept that fact from your substitute Uncle Mony.'

David looked relieved.

'Do you feel better?' I asked.

'I believe so,' he answered seriously.

A sweet, sensitive thirteen-year-old boy. A young gentleman in his

Bar Mitzvah outfit. No longer a child, not yet an adult. The beautiful but difficult age in between holding his future in his own hands.

'Why does everybody call you *Partners in Crime*?' David asked Mony. 'You never committed a crime, did you?'

Mony searched for the right words.

'Yes we did, David. Collectively and repeatedly. The worst possible crime.'

'What was that?' he asked.

'We were having fun. That was the crime. At home that was not allowed nor understood. We had fun at our meetings, and told our parents that we were there for educational reasons, to learn about Israel and the Middle East. Our parents tried their best to make us happy but it never really worked.'

'My dad told me about that,' said David. 'I've seen an old black and white picture. My father as a small child, together with my grandfather on the beach, trying to have fun. My grandfather was digging a hole, dressed in a three-piece suit and necktie. They both look so sad in that picture. My father also told me that they used to go on holidays, taking car trips to France and Switzerland. My grandparents thought that was fun for their child, but it wasn't. He would sit in the backseat and polish the chrome ashtray over and over again. He didn't see where they were going. Early in the day they checked into a hotel because my grandparents always took a nap in the afternoon. In his room dad was bored to tears. He would have preferred to stay home and play with his friends. My grandma always rented a small bungalow in the mountains. My grandparents spent all their time reading on the balcony. Books about the war that made them cry. They still cry sometimes.'

One of the guests who was about to leave offered David a ride home. David made a round of goodbyes and walked out the door.

'See you later, new *Partner in Crime*,' said Mony. 'Now you know our big secret so you are part of the gang.' David responded by sticking his thumb up to Mony.

'It's a little bit sad to see him go,' Rachel said. 'The next time we'll see him he won't be a child anymore. Like saying goodbye to his childhood. So long, child.'

'It's not sad for him,' Dave said. 'He will keep good memories of his childhood, his home, today. He is at a difficult age. That's all. Max, Gaby and David communicate. Today via Mony, but there's nothing wrong with that.'

'Maybe you are right,' I said. 'What a world of difference from the way we grew up. My dad would have killed me. He would have counted the number of rules I had violated, named them all in one indictment. My mother would have sentenced me to the death penalty without parole. One strike like that and I would have been out.'

'We more or less got that punishment anyhow,' said Fred. 'My dad would have called me a "schwindler".'

'That's exactly what you are,' Michael responded.

'To a certain extent I learned to lie,' Fred continued. 'My parents constantly felt that I didn't perform according to their expectations. They became desperate and so did I. Each time they imposed stricter rules. The more rules, the better. I couldn't cope with it, especially their verbal outbursts. That way I learned to lie.'

'I guess we all got screwed up by the rules,' Sally said. 'Obsession and rules were probably the only guidance they had to hold on to. Rules and unrealistic expectations. I could never do anything right in my entire life because I never could meet their expectations.'

'My parents always looked at me as if I was continuously committing crimes,' said Michael. 'I guess they were right too. I just didn't understand their system. We had rules and regulations for everything. When to have breakfast, coffee, tea, lunch, dinner. It was like a daily schedule that made the operation of the Swiss Rail System look like a complete mess. Everything was precisely counted. My mother knew exactly how many slices of bread there were, how many matzos, how many cookies, how many candies. When I was hungry between meals and took a peanut butter sandwich, I threw her entire bookkeeping system off and she became furious. That was a major violation, as if someone had stolen food. Actually she constantly thought that people were stealing from her. There was something missing all the time and she always accused someone. I once took a girlfriend home when my parents went out of town for a long weekend. The neighbors, who by the way collaborated with the Germans during the war, found it against their Christian morals that the girl stayed overnight and told my parents. Thanks to these peeks I was grounded for three months. A few weeks later my mother discovered a necklace "missing." She told my father that she was sure that my girlfriend had stolen it. 'Precisely the type, who does that kind of thing,' I heard her say. She had seen that girl maybe once or twice, briefly. My father promptly agreed. He called the girl's parents and threatened to report their daughter to the police if she wouldn't confess to her crime. Of course she didn't and did not know what all the verbal abuse was about. I've never seen her since She had enough of me and my family. That was the first and the last time I took a girlfriend home. Months later my mother found the necklace, some place where she had put it herself, hidden, because in her eyes every delivery person or repair man was a potential thief. I asked her to apologize to my girlfriend's parents.

"Are you out of your mind," she answered. "If you hadn't slept with that slut in our house nothing would have happened to begin with," she bitched at me. Later she became so paranoid that she continuously moved her jewelry to different hiding places. Once she returned from a vacation and she claimed that it had all been stolen. I was suspect number one. She and my dad gave me the third degree and then called the police. I was taken in for questioning. My mother filed an insurance claim and was promptly reimbursed a large sum of money. Weeks later she found all of her valuables in the attic where she had hidden them in an old suitcase.'

'She got you arrested?' asked Esther.

'Yes,' Michael answered. 'But it was not just me. We had several cleaning ladies who were fired on the spot, being accused of theft. Every time she filed charges. Needless to say that she was not the most popular client at the police station.'

'Is she still that paranoid?' Esther asked.

'It only becomes worse,' Michael explained. 'That kind of fear is highly contagious. They made my own wife freak out. A while back they invited her for the Sabbath meal because I was out of town for a few days. She told them about a bill collector who knocked on our door over an invoice I refused to pay. My parents totally panicked and told her that they could empty the house while she was gone. She knew that wasn't true, however, right after dinner she rushed home, almost in tears. She couldn't understand why my parents had scared her so much. I explained to her that during the war most of their belongings had been stolen. Prior to their deportation a gentile neighbor had offered to hide some of the silverware and books. When they returned from Poland in 1945, they went to that neighbor. He slammed the door in their faces. My mother kept yelling and banging on their door. She heard the neighbor's wife in the house asking what was going on.

"That fucking young Jewish couple from next door came back," the neighbor yelled at his wife. She opened a window on the second floor and calmly explained that times had been tough and unfortunately they had been forced to sell everything.

"What difference does it make." she said. "If you had not dumped all that junk with us, the Nazis would have taken it all anyhow. How could we know that you would come back. We thought you were dead, like all the others. And, don't forget, hiding all of these Jewish symbols was dangerous. You have no idea how scary it has been here while you were gone. We have also suffered a lot because of you Jews."

After saying this she shut the window. They have told me this story hundreds of times. Police officers were not very impressed or responsive when they reported the theft. Almost everybody had been stealing from the Jews, including the police.

"They all come here to complain about theft," an officer said. "It would be impossible for us to trace. I assume that the goods are no longer insured so it doesn't make sense to file a complaint. Besides, you voluntarily placed them with your neighbor and you have no receipt to show that the stuff was yours."

Michael's father argued that their household had been insured.

"We always paid our premium," he said.

"Not while you were gone," the policeman answered. "Or can you show me a policy or proof of payment?"

Michael's wife understood the explanation. But since the day his parents scared her she never visited them again.

'The same thing happened more or less to my parents,' I said.

'After the war my mother met the former housekeeper of her

parents. She was wearing her deceased mother's dress. She even wanted back payment.

"I kept the house in order while you were gone," she told my mother. "You owe me for that."

The entire interior had been sold.

'It happened to my parents,' said Fred.

'To most of them,' Mony said. 'None of us can imagine how it must have felt to be stripped of your belongings and dignity; standing nude in the cold, in front of a uniformed sadist. Surviving, returning home, finding your beloved ones gone. Perished in the camps. Goods stolen, bank accounts and savings stripped. And on top of that, most people found it a burden that Jews survived, returned and needed housing. The Holocaust didn't stop when the war ended. For our parents the misery continued.'

'For me too,' Michael said. 'Each night I dream that we'll lose everything and will be deported.'

'The only time that I really lost everything I had, was just before I moved in with Leslie,' said Dave. 'I was living with a girl in a shabby apartment in Amsterdam. She made a little money. I was supposed to attend university, but in fact I was only chasing girls. One day she saw me with another girl and you know what she did?'

'She treated you to an Alaska cruise to rescue the relationship,' said Fred.

'Close,' Dave continued. 'I came walking home from the pub with only two quarters left in my pocket. As I tried to get in I discovered that she had changed the locks and she had put a small bag with my clothes outside. Plus the keys to my dented wreck, one of these crummy post war vehicles that stalled all the time. I drove to a pay phone to call home, but the hysterical bitch hung up on me. I had one quarter left so I decided to call a friend of mine to ask if I could spend the night. I dialed a wrong number. My last quarter was gone. When I started to walk in the direction of my car, I discovered that it had been stolen. I had absolutely nothing, except for the clothes I was wearing.'

'That's how I got him,' Leslie said. 'At three in the morning. Broke and pale from all the girls he slept with. Now Sir Dave only flies first class and feels that he is too good for this hotel because the suites are too small. Thanks to him we don't stay with you in this hotel, but in the penthouse of some ridiculous fake palace, costing a bloody fortune, just to sleep for a few hours.'

'It's better like that,' Dave responded. 'Now I can work and make overseas phone calls at night without disturbing you.'

'Nonsense,' Leslie reacted. 'When I am asleep nothing wakes me up. You could fire a gun next to my pillow. You know that.'

'Even when I think that I might disturb you, it makes me feel uncomfortable. When I conduct business, I need to feel free to talk out loud, smoke a cigar, have a scotch. I need that privacy. You know that.'

'You are full of it,' said Leslie and kissed her husband.

The phone rang. Michael picked it up. With a monotone but friendly voice he said: 'Thank you for calling the *Partners in Crime*. All of our representatives are currently busy. Please hold the line. A gang member will answer your call shortly. If you want to make a donation, dial one, if you…'

Max interrupted him to tell us that David wanted to invite us the next morning for breakfast at the hotel.

'I hired a photographer to take a few pictures,' he said. 'Sounds stupid but it may be the last time we have this whole group together. Look what happened to Daisy. One day we'll all be gone.'

'So we'll take a picture and off we go, as if nothing happened?' Mony said.

'That's the way it is,' said Fred. 'We all have to go home, back to our families and to work except for this bum here,' pointing at me.

Michael asked Fred to play a few more songs. Together we sang old Israeli tunes that we used to sing during our clubhouse meetings. A little after three o'clock everyone left for their rooms. Tired and satisfied.

Rachel stayed behind.

'You want me to stay with you?' she asked.

I did.

'I'll be right back,' she said.

While she was gone I cleaned up the room a bit.

'Goodbye to David's childhood,' I whispered to myself. 'Goodbye *Partners in Crime*.'

For years we had been hanging on to a few happy memories that we shared. Brief moments of peace, emotional freedom and harmony. Maybe that was the only happiness in our childhoods that had not been ruined by the smell of death. Perhaps those were the only happy memories ever? All kids had loved their parents, their parents had loved them. So how come my father never hugged or kissed me? And that my mother only did after she had hit me? The other *Partners in Crime* had not been physically abused, but they all got an overdose of what they didn't want and they didn't get what they needed. They were exceptional people, raised by damaged parents who had lost most or all of their relatives.

Most of the *Partners in Crime* eventually managed to establish good relationships. Not easy on the spouses but that is not essential, as long as it works.

'Goodbye contaminated, early gray generation,' I talked to myself in the mirror. 'Now pass on the relay stick to David and his friends.' I stuck my tongue out to my reflection in the mirror.

'Do you like what you see?' asked Rachel, who had returned with her suitcase.

'I have no clue,' I answered.

'I do,' she said and kissed me.

'Are you moving in with me?' I asked, pointing at her suitcase.

'I haven't used my own room since I checked into this hotel, so I might as well move in, as you call it.'

'It is very sweet of you to stay with me,' I said. 'The nights haven't been all that pleasant over the past months.'

'It is not exactly a sacrifice,' Rachel answered. 'What have you been doing all night, all this time you were unable to sleep?'

'I have been watching television, drinking and smoking too much and listening to the radio until I fall asleep on the couch or the floor for a few hours.'

'Did you try..?'

I interrupted her.

'I tried everything, believe me. Yoga, sleeping pills, liquor. Nothing worked. The days have been bearable, the nights are still a punishment.'

I put Rachel's suitcase on the bed and she started to unpack.

'What is it that you are thinking about at night?'

'I wish I knew,' I answered. 'Flashes of memories, worries, things I need to do. As soon as I try to relax it happens.'

'Is it all connected to Daisy?' Rachel asked.

'Rarely. Many of these thoughts have already turned into happy memories. I saw a film the other day about losing a spouse. Just before she died she said that the happy moments now, were going to be the sadness of the future. I don't believe that is true. Happy moments always turn into good memories. It's only a matter of time.'

Rachel walked into the bathroom and put all of her toiletries and make-up on the marble counter.

'Create more, new endearing moments,' she said. 'All of these moments will turn into happy memories. We all need them to overshadow the bad ones. Maybe we should all say Kaddish for the deceased, the past, the smell of death, the anxiety, for being accused of stealing the unrealistic expectations of our parents, for the obnoxious rules of the houses where we grew up, for everything that was mentioned here tonight and yesterday.'

While saying this she had started to undress, put her clothes on a hanger and her underwear in a laundry bag.

Rachel took a shower. I started to prepare myself for the night, washed my face and body with a cold, wet towel, brushed my teeth, put on a robe and sat down on the sofa to read a newspaper. I was interrupted by Rachel's touch. She looked gorgeous in her silky, sexy nightgown. She sat down next to me. Her wet, long, dark hair smelled of flowers. She put her head on my shoulder.

'We are going to fill you up with happy moments and good memories for later,' she whispered in my ear. 'That's a promise.' She fondled my hair.

I enjoyed her presence. Her breath, her warm breasts pressed into my body. It relaxed me completely. I sighed a couple of times and almost fell asleep.

'You see that you still can relax and fall asleep?' she said. 'The only thing that it takes is a little bit of love. Come, let's go to bed.'

She took my hand and walked me to the bed. I laid down. Rachel turned the lights off. She left the light in the bathroom on and the door half open.

'This way I can look at you,' she said.

She snuggled next to me, took my hand, put it under her nightgown as an invitation to satisfy her. She quietly enjoyed our lovemaking, had two orgasms shortly after another. She then put her arms around me and we fell asleep.

17

Rachel's soft lips woke me up in the morning. She silently stared at me with her loving face, her black shiny hair leaning on the white pillow. I closed my eyes again to enjoy the delight of the moment.

'You know that I never had an orgasm with a man before,' she said.

'Good morning to you too,' I answered.

'Seriously,' she proceeded. 'I have masturbated a lot. Isaac only raped me. It hurt, turned me off and paralyzed me. The smell of his rancid sweaty body and his bad breath made me nauseous. I used to turn my head away and tried to think of something else. Like watering the roses in the garden, or I tried to memorize a recipe for ginger cookies. Fortunately he fucked like a rabbit so he was through in a matter of minutes but they felt like hours. I was squeezing the frame of the bed as hard as I could and cramped my toes so that pain distracted me. I was always hoping that one month he would forget, but that never happened. Each month he carefully counted the days until I had my ovulation. He called it a woman's duty and for a while I believed that, like a burden women have to live with.

When I became pregnant I lied, telling him that the doctor had urged me not to have sex during pregnancy and up to three months after childbirth. I loved being pregnant. One year without that monthly torture. He was the first and only man in my life, I couldn't let any man come close to me after what happened. I had no one I could talk to about all that, except for you.'

'I don't recall any conversation on that subject,' I said.

'Well we talked. Maybe to you it was like any normal conversation that you don't recall. To me it was shocking what you said.'

'What? Did I traumatize your poor, innocent soul? In case you are trying to give me the guilt trip you are wasting your valuable time.'

'You told me that everybody must do whatever he wants, as long as both enjoy sex, you don't end up with an unwanted pregnancy or get infected by a nasty disease. Now it only sounds rational to me, back then it was shocking to me. In my environment sex was not a subject to be openly discussed with women. Of course I thought about it a lot, I had my desires but I didn't know what to do. I fantasized, masturbated. I enjoyed that a lot, but when a man came close I totally froze.

'You didn't seem to have that problem last night,' I said.

'You know that's something else,' Rachel replied. 'You're not a man.'

'What? You want me to teach you about the birds and the bees?'

'Oh, don't drivel. You know what I mean. You are like family, like a big brother or so.'

'Nice brother,' I said. 'Grabbing my little, innocent sister. You know what happens when you sleep with your brother? You get weird creatures like in remote areas. Where there is only incest because they look askance at any stranger, if they ever come in town. You are afraid of men, but you love incest?'

Rachel stopped me talking by putting her finger on my mouth.

'Don't spoil this precious moment with stupid remarks,' she said. 'This is beautiful, the nicest beginning of a new day. My big brother took me into the swimming pool, showed me how to swim and taught me that deep water isn't dangerous.'

'Don't go overboard now and just plunge into any pool,' I said. 'There may be sharks in there, you know. Your finger may be safer.'

'Were you comfortable playing with me last night?' she shyly asked.

'Comfortable isn't the right word,' I answered. 'We made love and enjoyed every moment. Maybe we are in a similar situation. Not that I was ever raped like you were. But I lost my appetite for sex since I became a widower. After Daisy died I masturbated on thoughts of the deceased with my feet on the cold tiles, dropping my sperm on the bathroom floor.'

'What a waste,' Rachel said.

'Not completely,' I responded. 'Ants eat sperm. Several times I saw a long line of ants enjoying what I had just produced. Like lining up for the automatic teller of a sperm bank. I was addicted to Daisy. When she died I was forced to go cold turkey. After a while the lust was gone.'

'That's not what I have learned,' Rachel responded. 'If you quit smoking and you light a cigarette after ten years, you're hooked again. Addictions are lifelong.'

'You may be right,' I said. 'I don't like sharing my bedroom with anyone anymore. To me it feels like being a ship without a safe harbor. Only being with you seems to be permitted.'

'Mandatory,' she said while she put herself on top of me. Again we made passionate love after which we comfortably rested in each other's arms.

'We have learned two things,' she said after a while. 'Your old body parts are still intact and I seem to be capable of enjoying making love, despite my age. We both are pre-owned but in mint condition. I am sure you are going to run into someone again whom you will spoil rotten, even more than Daisy.'

'She never objected,' I said.

'You bet she didn't,' Rachel said. 'But you were the emotional provider. What's wrong with you men? You marry a darling or a bitch. It doesn't matter. You do anything to please them. Maybe you guys try to please your spouses' because you never succeeded pleasing your parents. I don't know. But you too deserve to be spoiled. Maybe it sounds harsh but facts are fact. Daisy died almost a year ago. That chapter is closed forever and you have to get on with your life. She is no longer with us. That's cruel. Yet you have the duty to take good care of yourself and lead a happy life. I lost a lot too. My family doesn't speak to me anymore and I've lost my children. You and your gang members got me back on my feet, now I'm lying next to you. Without these horrible events we would not be here in bed together.'

'I don't think that you necessarily need to suffer to become a happy person,' I said.

'Don't tell me that you expect life to be fair,' Rachel continued. 'You can't change what happened in the past. It's too late. Molly lost her son. Our parents lost their families. Our families. Daisy's body was dragged out of a car wreck. It's not fair and we deserve better. Our parents had to carry on, without support of anyone. You are named after two dead grandfathers. You have to carry that weight, maybe feel comfortable or proud about it, but you cannot hold on to them. If you lay your head down on a picture of the deceased, it's cold. If you try to constantly touch the past, you miss out on the warm parking place of living and loving, be it my shoulder or another one, with different perfume and maybe blond hair, if that's what you want. It feels a lot better than living out of a suitcase in hotels, putting your head on a cold pillow and waking up alone. That's how I feel and you can't tell me that you are any different.'

At eight o'clock my brother Eric called. He offered to pick me up later to go see a matinee with Molly and her husband Boy. I filled up the bathtub with hot water and bubbles from a pink, plastic container in the shape of a champagne bottle. Rachel asked me to come back to bed.

'Let's snuggle up for a few more minutes,' she said. 'Now it's all endearing and peaceful. Shortly we have to step into the real harsh world again.'

The phone rang again.

'Let it ring,' Rachel said. 'I don't want anybody to disturb us now and take this nice moment away. We deserve a little privacy.'

We relaxed in each other's arms. The best thinkable beginning of a new day to be enjoyed as long as possible. Just as we comfortably sat down in the bathtub together someone knocked on the door. The **Do Not Disturb** sign was on the door handle so we decided not to be disturbed.

I washed Rachel's body from top to toe.

'Take your time,' she said. 'Breakfast is not until nine thirty anyhow and this feels much better than the mikva.' She laid back in the foamy, hot water and wet her hair.

'You are very sweet to me,' she said. 'I've never felt this good before. Maybe I shouldn't but I need to share a secret with you.'

'Once you share a secret it is no longer a secret but public information,' I responded.

'I don't care,' said Rachel as she poured shampoo on her hair.

'All these years, since we met, I've been fantasizing about you when I was masturbating. I felt guilty about it because you didn't know and I felt that I was cheating on Daisy somehow. Now it feels a little bit like I am cheating on a dead friend.'

'Don't accuse yourself of a crime you did not commit,' I said. 'What I'd like to know is, what was better, your fantasies or reality?'

I'll probably never know the answer to this question, because at that moment the door opened and Fred shamelessly walked straight into the bathroom. Instead of apologizing for disturbing our privacy he started ranting.

'Good morning,' he said with a beaming face. 'I tried to call you and I knocked on your door but you didn't answer.'

'Maybe that's because we didn't want to be disturbed,' I answered. 'Did you ever try to realize what it means when people put that red sign on their doorknob?'

Fred did not answer and sat down on the toilet, lighting a cigarette.

'I got smashed last night,' he said. 'I went out.'

'In the middle of the night?' Rachel interrupted him. 'You're nuts. It was at least after three o'clock when you left.'

'That's correct,' Fred smiled. 'I went to the lobby to see if there was still something going on. There I ran into a gorgeous woman. I invited her for a drink but of course the bar was closed. She then invited me to her room for a nightcap. We had great sex.'

'And?' Rachel asked.

'That is the last thing I remember,' Fred explained. 'She poured a couple of drinks. She must have drugged me, because I woke up an hour ago with a splitting headache.'

'And your new fiancée had vanished?' Rachel asked. 'The magical disappearance trick?'

'Bingo,' Fred admitted. 'But she didn't leave alone. She left accompanied by my wallet, my money, passport and return ticket to Amsterdam.'

'Is there any occasion where you don't shoot yourself in your foot?' I asked.

'What do you mean?' he asked with a fake innocent expression on his face.

'What I mean is that nobody in his right mind gets himself invited by a hooker in the middle of the night. You're not that naive. You knew precisely what you were up to,' I irritably responded. 'Your mammy gave you permission to go abroad for a few days. You get smashed, lose your dignity and all of your personal belongings, maybe you come home with some horrible, transmittable disease. On top of that you have the chutzpah to invite yourself into my room, sit down on my toilet while Rachel and I are bathing and bother us with all that tasteless crap.'

'Well, let me explain...' said Fred.

I interrupted him. 'I am not interested in your heroic tales. You probably cheated the woman at the front desk out of a spare key with a baloney story, telling her that you are my twin brother or best friend who wanted to surprise me for my birthday. You could use a good shrink. If you want to consult me you can come see me first thing after breakfast. Now, get lost.'

'After breakfast I need to go to the Dutch consulate-general to arrange for a new passport, to a travel agent to get a new airline ticket, to the police to report the theft so maybe my travel insurance will cover something.'

'So are you going to make up yet another story to cheat your insurance agent?' Rachel asked. 'You make life so complicated with all these lies. Ever consider to just behave like an adult and tell the truth?'

'I wish you good luck at the consulate,' I said. 'It's Sunday.'

'Shit, well maybe I'll stay a few days longer in New York,' he responded. 'It's a virtue of need. Talking about needs. A friend in need is a friend indeed. I need to borrow some money for taxis and so on. I am dead broke.'

'I'd rather give it to you,' I responded. 'I don't want to run the risk that I get your wife on the line, two years from now, having to ask her to reimburse me for the unhappy hooker incident in New York. My wallet is in my jacket. Take a few hundred dollars and we'll never talk about it again.'

Fred left the room, happily whistling.

The unhappy hooker incident was not over for him. A few months later he called me telling me that he had infected his wife with a venereal disease. She banned him to a small guestroom in their attic. For the first time telling stories and making things up did not work. He was forced to speak the truth. He didn't like that. Neither did his wife who filed for divorce.

Rachel put her make-up on while I dressed.
'What are you going to do after everyone leaves today?' I asked her.
'Hang around the city perhaps,' she answered. 'I have an open ticket so I can leave whenever I want to and I don't have to work for the next two weeks.'
'Would you like to join me on a short trip to the West Coast?' I suggested.
'Where are you going?' she asked.
'To La Jolla,' I answered. 'That's where I have been living these past few months. It's a great place. Maybe I am going to settle there. The weather is good, it's a cute village full of short skirted, dyed blond, southern California girls driving around in their German convertibles.
They never ask you who you are, but what you are worth. They look for an unrealistic dream come true, hoping to run into a rich, single surgeon who will buy them a big house with an ocean view and take them to conventions in Paris and Tokyo.'

'What are the men looking for?' Rachel asked curiously.

'The men are only looking at themselves. They love themselves. They are lifting weights in front of a mirror at their gym, taking steroids to build big strong muscles, getting nice dark skin at the tanning salon so they don't look pale when they go to the beach. They wear iPod earphones and chew gum. Basically they are lazy, they don't need all these muscles and they hunt for easy targets. Women whose biological clock starts to tick, who are almost forty, haven't met the wealthy surgeon yet and are ready to settle for less. A roof, a baby and a couple of credit cards. They get stuck with such a body builder. A schlemiel stockbroker who has to get up every morning at three o'clock to drive to his office before the New York Stock Exchange opens. After work he comes home and immediately falls asleep on the sofa until five, when he and his pals meet at the gym and go have a beer in a noisy pub, watching baseball on television because they have nothing to discuss. When he comes home, a little before nine, he goes directly to bed and falls asleep.'

'Do they ever make love in southern California?' Rachel teased.

'Only when there is a power outage after an earthquake,' I said. 'Or when the TV breaks down. On Saturday's there is no time for sex because the entire population gathers in malls to buy things that they don't need, like beepers and cellular phones for their infants. On Sunday's men go to ballgames and come home drunk. On national holidays they go see family, barbecue and get stuck on the freeways, so actually there is never time for the intimate act. Except for singles. They meet in sleazy bars whenever the urge arises. The women look like princesses, but the next morning in bright daylight when their hair is back into natural shape, they've taken off their push-up bras, walk around in shorts, in sneakers, they look like housewives. Who wants that?'

'I wouldn't,' Rachel responded. 'There must be something that attracts you, otherwise you would not have spent so much time out there. I'll take you up on your offer because I'd like to see what it is.'

She looked at her watch. 'It's almost breakfast time,' she said. 'Let's go downstairs.

Hand in hand we walked to the elevator. I felt comfortable with Rachel. We were able to talk, laugh, enjoy life together. She was pretty and smartly dressed. The best company I could have wished for.

I shared my thoughts with her.

'Not bad for two damaged kids in their mid-life crisis,' she responded.

Downstairs in the restaurant Fred was proudly telling the others about his nightly adventures. He was obviously enjoying the attention and glorified his story in a humorous manner. Everybody was laughing.

The photographer that Max had arranged for arrived. He took pictures and ran off to have them processed, so we could each take a copy before the end of breakfast.

Fred, Michael, Sally, Phil and Joan, Esther, Mony, Rachel, Max and Gaby, Dave and Leslie, me, and our new *Partner in Crime*, David.

Another hour and we would say goodbye to each other and also to a part of our youth. No more meetings that had brought us together, summer camps from where nobody wanted to go home, no more parties and dialogues in my hotel room. The stories about the homes where we grew up, the depressed, anxious and often angry parents who had lost everything and everybody. People who were forced to walk a "march of death" and accidentally survived. They were all still alive due to coincidence. Now, leaving New York, it felt like the end of an era to the *Partners in Crime*.

No one said much during breakfast. It felt unreal. The last sixty minutes of the *Partners in Crime* era was spent eating scrambled eggs and drinking coffee? The last minutes of the last camp ticking away? Again, no one wanted to leave and say goodbye. Max tried to thank us but got stuck in an attempt delivering a speech. Tears streaming from his eyes. He was saved by the photographer who came back with our group pictures. A smiling bunch of middle aged people, photographed together for the first and the last time.

I thanked Gaby, Max and David for the invitation for the wonderful Bar Mitzvah, for providing the opportunity to get together. For the endearing memories and the unique picture that we would take home as a precious token of a very special occasion, a weekend we would never forget.

'Especially Fred,' Michael added. 'He'll remember, taking all his crab lice home. Nice present for his wife and cheap too. Let's go into town and buy some presents for our families.

Rachel joined them. Later she would try to get some rest. I took a stroll through the neighborhood until I would meet my brother Eric.

18

Eric was pulling into the hotel driveway while talking on his cell phone. My sitting down next to him hardly interrupted him. He kept talking on the phone.

'Yes sweetie, I know. I am running late. I just picked up my brother, I still have to get the tickets to the show on the West Side so I really don't have time to go to the grocery store. Can't you just… yes I know, sweetie, I should have left home earlier.'

The conversation continued until he finally surrendered and promised to go to the grocery store on the way home to pick up his wife. She refused to take a train to the city, making Eric spend hours fighting traffic in the New York area.

He asked me how the Bar Mitzvah had been.

'Very special,' I answered. 'An unforgettable meeting. Too bad you couldn't make it.'

'I don't have time for that kind of nonsense,' he responded. 'I'm working around the clock and besides, I don't see the point of wasting a weekend with people I hardly remember. It doesn't mean anything to me anymore and I hate to go to temple. I can't sit still for such a long time, it's too slow for me. Everybody goes so slowly, everyone is slow. It's getting at me. How come I am always the first one to arrive or to be through with work? Shit, I'm in the wrong lane. Damn it, and the next street is one way into the wrong direction. I'll never make it in time. Do you know how to get back from here?'

The phone rang.

'No sweetie, I'm still down town and... shit, now I am stuck on 47th Street.... Yes, I'll try to hurry up sweetie....'

I tuned out and tried to enjoy the ride through Manhattan.

Eric continued to curse, change lanes and told me all about the car he was driving.

'I love four wheel drives,' he explained. 'Other cars don't block your view and in a collision I am sitting high and dry. A great engine too. She accelerates like a rocket. Japanese but ninety-five percent manufactured in the United States. I only buy American.'

When we finally arrived at his home his wife was waiting for us with a warm reception.

'You're late,' she snapped. 'The next time you make me wait I'll order a limo.'

'I couldn't help it, sweetie,' Eric defended himself. 'We got stuck in traffic. I simply couldn't move any faster.'

She turned her back on him indicating that she expected him to help her into her mink coat. Meanwhile she talked to me. 'So since you are single you are partying again, I've heard. Well, why not? There is nothing wrong with enjoying yourself as a bachelor. You're right, I guess. You only live once. Your brother never quit behaving like a bachelor. It would have been cheaper if he had gone to a hooker once a week and less humiliating for me.'

'Please don't do this,' Eric tried to interrupt her. 'You don't need to keep bringing that up.'

She walked off to the front door and bitched, 'One more word about it and I'll file for divorce.'

'Say that one magic word,' I whispered into Eric's ear as we followed his wife. 'Say it and you're a free man.'

Eric opened the passenger side front door for Irene.

'You know I'll sue you for all you've got,' she added.

'Maybe you better swallow that one word,' I whispered to him.

As we drove back to Manhattan she made it clear that we had a new captain on board.

'Change lanes to the right now. Now! No, now you're too late. Go right, right,' she commanded. 'No, not here, we'll get stuck at the toll bridge.'

When it came down to finding a parking spot she suddenly waived her responsibilities as a commanding officer. As we approached the theater she said, 'Just drop me off in front of the entrance. I don't want to walk through that filthy snow slush.'

We met Boy and Molly at a restaurant close to the theatre. Boy got his first name from a Dutch farmer who hid him from 1943 until 1945. His real name was Abraham but he never used it. A small resistance unit that had found him a place to hide, provided him with a new, non-Jewish identity. His name on his new ID was Wilhelm de Wit. The farmer called him Boy because he didn't like Wilhelm as a name. It sounded too German to him so he tried to find an English name that was acceptable in his local dialect.

'Abraham is a boy,' he had reasoned. 'A sweet, big boy. So we'll call you Boy.'

Boy was ten when his parents left him with two men who were members of a small, communist resistance group. He realized that he would probably not see his parents and two younger sisters again.

The two men took Boy on a long bike ride from Amsterdam to the farmland in the northern part of Holland. It was freezing cold and uncomfortable. The bicycles had no tires, due to a shortage of supplies caused by Hitler's war machine. Numbed by storm and snow they struggled on. They were stopped several times by Dutch police. The two men had good quality falsified papers and got permission to proceed. Until they reached a German road block. Boy was separated from the two men who were taken into a small shack for questioning. Boy was put into the back of an army truck, scared and shivering from cold. He didn't understand much German but realized that this was bad news.

A middle aged German soldier asked for his name. Boy didn't answer. The soldier walked off but returned after a few minutes with a long, heavy army coat, a blanket and two candy bars.

'Here, take this my child,' he said in Dutch with a strong German accent.

'I have children too, you know. And a home, somewhere. Maybe I'll never see my family again. Or I get killed, or the Russians will occupy my hometown. We both deserve better than this.'

He walked to the little shack. Boy heard him curse in German.

'Fuck your bureaucracy,' he yelled. 'We are losing the war and you let that boy outside die of pneumonia?'

Somebody answered but Boy couldn't hear what they said. The soldier cursed again.

'Papers, papers, fucking papers. You have so many papers and forms that you can't tell one from another anymore. Of course your papers never match. The hell with it. Let these men go and take care of that little boy.'

Shortly afterwards the men came out and put Boy on the back of a bike.

'That was a terrifying close call,' he heard one whisper to the other.

After another day riding through snowstorms, they safely reached Boy's new hiding place. The two men left him in the hands of the farmer who had properly prepared for his arrival. He took good care of Boy. For emergency cases there was a small hiding spot underneath the pig stables.

'A door in the ground, underneath the stables, covered with pig shit,' as he described it. 'Whenever shit was approaching, I had to go through that shit door and cover myself with pig shit.'

The area was searched several times. Boy had to disappear in his small, smelly, cold and dark hiding spot. On one occasion he heard soldiers walking right over his hiding place. He was scared to be discovered and even more that they would fire into the ground. The German soldiers stayed close to the farm for two days so Boy had to stay underground. Finally, when the farmer released him, Boy was puking from fear and the smell of pig shit and of his own excrement. He was dehydrated and suffered from a high fever.

The farmer secretly listened to the Dutch radio transmissions from London during which speeches were delivered by Queen Wilhelmina who had fled during the German invasion. Her daughter Juliana lived safe and sound in Canada. At some point during the occupation the Nazis ordered possession of radios illegal, but many people kept one anyway. The farmer was indignant at the Queen's speeches.

'She fails to mention the faith of the Jews or to encourage the Dutch to hide them,' he complained. 'The royal family extremely disappoints me.'

Sometimes Boy was allowed to play with the son of the Minister of the local Christian Reform Church. The child, about Boy's age, needed shelter periodically. His father frequently went to the police station after roundups. As often as he could he picked up a few children. He told the policemen that they belonged to his Church congregation and were not Jewish. He took them home and rapidly had to find a hiding place for them. He usually succeeded via his contacts with a resistance unit. His son Steve then had to stay with the farmer where Boy was in hiding, because the Minister didn't want to take the risk to endanger his son. Steve told Boy that his father had been arrested several times. Once he stayed away for three days and when he returned his hands were wrapped in bloody bandages. During the interrogations by the Gestapo his fingernails had been pulled out one by one to make him talk, which he didn't. He was released and courageously continued his brave mission to save as many children as he could.

After the liberation in 1945, Boy returned to the area where he used to live. His house was no longer there. The only survivor in his family was an uncle who hated children. After having been bawled at for over a year, a social worker placed him in an orphanage.

There he met Molly. She hardly ever talked about the Holocaust. All I knew was that she and a brother where the sole survivors of a big family. She was a strong woman with a great sense of humor. Only when there was a television program on with pictures of a concentration camp did she cry and say: 'I know, I was there.'

Both Boy and Molly worked hard and never complained. They raised three children with great joy until the youngest died. It was as if all the sadness of their lives was suddenly released. They were heart-stricken. They were mourning for their child and many others they had loved and lost.

Boy and I took endless walks. He used to cry continuously, which he did not want to do at home, telling me how guilty he felt that he had not been able to save anyone, one of his sisters, or now his own child.

'Maybe if I had paid more attention, watched him more closely. Maybe....' A thousand maybe's.

Molly sat at home, sheltering from the world. After a long and painful struggle they coped with the harsh reality, but their cheerfulness never revived.

'During the day I think of him, at night he still is in my dreams,' Molly said.

The loss of their child almost destroyed their marriage. Boy's way to carry on was working day and night. Molly needed to talk a lot and stay home. They were unable to comfort each other. They hardly communicated, creating misunderstandings and arguments. Their anger about the indescribable injustice slowly vanished after years. The sadness remained, the marriage survived.

In an attempt to cheer each other up we created the habit of sending each other funny Cd's and books. We faxed good political cartoons from local newspapers, sent jokes per e-mail. Anything to create a smile. Whenever we had a chance to get together we went to a funny movie or a comedy on stage.

During this visit to New York we had tickets to a stage comedy, highly praised in a New York Times review. Rightfully so. I enjoyed the show but most of all hearing Boy and Molly's bursts of laughter. It had been such a long time.

After the show we dropped Boy and Molly off at their hotel. They were still giggling.

En route to my hotel Eric all of a sudden said: 'I take back what I said earlier. I would have liked to have been at David's Bar Mitzvah.'

'What a waste of time,' his wife said. 'You can't afford to get involved with these kind of things anymore. You have better things to do. Besides, you don't keep any happy memories of those years.'

'You're right, sweetie,' Eric answered. 'But I felt at home with these kids and we had so much in common.'

'Like what?'

'We all came from emotionally disturbed families, all of them Holocaust survivors.'

'My ass,' Irene responded. 'Your parents are simply jerks. Before and after the war.'

'Maybe,' Eric said. 'But had it been a normal family, perhaps I'd have had a nice uncle or aunt, a grandparent. Maybe I would have had a place to go to.'

'Horse shit,' Irene said. 'Your father told you himself that he hated his family, his own parents, brothers and sister. They were jerks too. None of them would have been nice to you. Lousy people are crap, with or without a war.'

'But under normal circumstances my father could have met a nice girl and would have been exposed to a caring family. That could have changed him. Instead he had to run and go into hiding. He had no chance to learn how to normally deal with people.'

'Nonsense,' Irene persisted. 'I don't think that the nicest people necessarily survived.'

'My mother's family was nice,' Eric tried.

'Give me a break,' Irene argued. 'Maybe so. That's why they did not survive. But your grandfather was a stupid butcher, a spineless chap who did nothing else but try to comfort his wife, who was an absolute bitch.'

'Maybe it runs in the family?' I contributed to the conversation.

For a minute there was complete silence.

'The parents were all so sad,' Eric finally continued.

'Do you remember Dicky?' he asked me. 'Such a sweet boy, such darling parents but always so incredibly sad. Maybe that's what we had in common. Sad parents, anxious, angry. All different kids with a similar past.'

'How are your children?' I asked.

'Oh well. Into their own business. They didn't even want to join us today. I guess they are with friends or at a disco.'

As Eric walked me into my hotel he apologized.

'I am sorry,' he said. 'I would have loved to come in for a minute but I'm in a hurry.'

His wife dramatized his statement by loudly honking the horn.

'Move,' she yelled. 'I am not going to sit here forever. I'm sick and tired of waiting for you.'

Time was up. Irene was ruling with an iron fist. A stopwatch in one hand and a rolling-pin in the other.

19

Rachel was waiting for me in my hotel room, chatting with Fred who was waiting to obtain a new passport and flight ticket. They were sharing a bottle of good wine.

'Was it fun or shouldn't we ask?' Fred inquired.

'The show was outstanding, Boy and Molly finally laughed again, my brother is working on his first heart attack just to maintain his status and Irene... Irene is Irene,' I summarized.

'We have been talking some more this afternoon,' Fred said. 'Just before everybody left.'

'About what?'

'About you and everybody.'

'Could we please skip the questions and answers?' I asked while Rachel poured me a glass of wine.

'We were talking about the *Partners in Crime* as a family. We all live so far apart.'

'So what do you want to do? Live together? Start some sort of cult in Waco, Texas? Daily prayer and community suicide? It's over, my friend. We always stayed in touch, but the old days are gone. We had a couple of nostalgic days but don't get stuck here. We said goodbye and everybody is going their own way again, back to business as usual.'

'That is the catch,' Rachel explained. 'It's always back to business as usual. We always need to fulfill our obligations and carry on. This weekend meant a lot more than a little partying. It showed how supportive we have been, how close a tie there is. So close that nobody had the courage to properly say goodbye this morning. We were all silent, staring gloomily at our scrambled eggs. Why? Because we touched lots of subjects, explaining who we are, the way it was, where we stand now, our shortcomings. All given facts, like Daisy was the first one to die on us. But we left a loose end. We talked for a couple of days but avoided saying goodbye. We never had a chance to say goodbye, to mourn for Daisy, mourn for the deceased or our depressive childhoods. Maybe if we mourn together once, we will be able to leave some of these smothering thoughts behind us. Did you say Kaddish for Daisy all these months?'

'Yes,' I answered. 'Like a religious man. I don't know why but I did and I will. It's been almost a year. I'll go to her grave once more in December and then I will do it long distance again like the past few months, providing that the Almighty will function as satellite.'

'Would it be alright with you if we join you in December?' Fred asked. 'So we can say goodbye to Daisy and say Kaddish for all the deceased we talked about.'

'Sounds like a ball to me,' I said. 'A posthumous surprise party for the remains of my wife, celebrating the anniversary of her death, to commemorate her pretty body being crunched. No, more than that. We'll make it into a private, exclusive *Partners in Crime* Memorial Day, including two minutes of silence. Then we raise the flag and sing the national anthem, followed by fireworks.

"Oh, Say, can you see, by the dawn's early light," I started to sing.

'No,' Fred interrupted me. 'On Memorial Day we could never really concentrate our thoughts, let alone mourn. I always tried to think about my parents' memories but of course that was impossible. The only thing that my father would say, were things like, "It's well done, this ceremony. Appropriate short speech by the mayor." But never a word about his thoughts or emotions.'

I closed my eyes for a minute to put Fred's words into perspective and what Rachel tried to get across. Daisy would have loved the thought that she could be of value after her death. Especially if that could lead to reconciliation and an improvement of the quality of life of her *Partners in Crime*. To me it could provide an opportunity, separating from her in a more honorable manner than with the last words that she said to me. "It's good for you." That was about ice-skating.

'If the others are for it, I am too,' I decided.

'Dave already anticipated that you would agree,' Rachel said. 'Tomorrow he will make travel arrangements for us all. He knows the owner of an excellent hotel. We can all stay there.'

'I will call him tomorrow,' I promised. 'We are on, December fifteenth.'

Fred was forced to spend the night in Rachel's room, being broke and without papers. Rachel and I discussed our plans in length until we fell asleep, early in the morning.

20

The first two days in La Jolla, Rachel and I just relaxed. The New York experience with the *Partners in Crime* had been wonderful but tiring with all the long talks until the middle of the night. Rachel slept most of the way from New York to San Diego.

I rearranged my briefcase, looking at some pictures. Dave, Leslie and I in San Francisco, and the *Partners in Crime*, united in New York. Endearing memories.

We arrived late, took a taxi to downtown La Jolla and checked in with the La Valencia hotel. A gorgeous resort with a breathtaking ocean view.

While Rachel took a bath, I went to a store to buy some snacks and wine so we could enjoy a light, late-night supper in our room.

The next morning we ate breakfast on our balcony, facing the Pacific. We read the newspapers, went out for a walk in the park, watched the seals, fed the birds and squirrels and observed people on their boats or snorkeling. We quietly spent the afternoon on the balcony, listening to the peaceful sound of the surf.

We were only interrupted once by a call from my mother.

'Your father is sick,' she told me. 'He hardly eats. He has lost so much weight. It is scary.'

For weeks she had tried to make him go see a doctor. When he finally did, an internist recommended a colon scan.

After he came home he searched through his medical encyclopedia.

'That quack talks nonsense,' he said. 'I won't let him stick a camera into my touchis to have him prove a point that he hasn't anyhow. It's the ulcer that I got during the war.'

He spent half the days in bed, refusing to follow the doctor's advice. Self medicating with pills, prescribed fifteen years earlier.

'When he is up, he just sits and reads. He hardly talks to me,' my mother complained.

I asked her if there was anything I could do for them.

'I wish you could,' she answered. 'He is so stubborn, especially when he is sick.'

To me it all sounded too familiar. He had always been impossible during illnesses. This situation sounded serious, though.

I wanted to be alone for a little bit to digest the information. I walked down the street, bought a postcard and sat down at a sidewalk coffee shop. I wrote a few notes to my brother Eric.

Worshipful and assiduous Brother,

Hopefully you and your family are well. I just had the privilege of receiving a phone call from mother dearest. Father is ill. It is unclear how serious because, as usual, he refuses to listen to his physician. I wish him good health until 120 years of age. However, we need to be realistic and face the fact that he will pass away one day. Perhaps you feel you need to consider what you need or want to do when he dies. Not an easy one to answer for you but important, I guess. I realize that all too well. But, my beloved, well respected, hard working brother, you and you alone have to spend the rest of your life with your own conscience.

Say hello to Irene and the children.

A hug from sunny La Jolla,

Your homeless brother.

I mailed the postcard. On the way back to the hotel I walked into an exclusive designer women's clothing store. Rachel had brought outfits for New York in the winter, not for a subtropical climate. I bought several sexy, glitzy summer dresses for her. For a few seconds I felt uncomfortable, buying clothes again for a woman, like I used to do for Daisy.

'Is it for your wife or a friend?' the saleswomen asked me.

'What's the difference?' I inquired.

'If it is for your wife the wrapping should look modest or she is going to kill you for spending all that money. If it is for a girlfriend it can't look expensive enough.'

'I bought it for myself,' I answered. 'Sometimes I like to dress like a woman.'

As I left she looked confused.

'I bought you some sexy clothes,' I said to Rachel as I returned to the hotel room. 'Nice for me to watch and you can now compete fairly with the short skirted locals.'

'I'm glad you did,' she said. 'Very considerate. I feel like a Jewish American Princess because the only things I did while you were gone, is washing my hair and making a reservation at the Top O' the Cove restaurant. We'll go there early to view the sunset and have dinner.'

At the restaurant we sat next to the window, looking at the sun go down into the deep blue ocean. After dinner we spent several hours listening to an entertainer at the piano bar adjoining the restaurant.

21

The next morning we witnessed a wedding in the courtyard of the hotel, looking down from a terrace where we were having coffee. It was a glamorous ceremony. The bride looked like Cinderella in her white, lace dress. The bridegroom like the doorman of the hotel, in his brand new tuxedo. The bridesmaids wore old fashioned shiny, pink, satin dresses like back in the Victorian era. Every move was orchestrated by a professional party planner and her two assistants, like on a Hollywood film set. Hundreds of guests looked like they had been invited to a gala with the Queen of England. There was an orchestra with violins, cellos, an organ and the courtyard was decorated with thousands of flowers.

Rachel watched silently.

'It doesn't look real,' Rachel said at the end of the ceremony. 'It's like what you would see in the old days, drippy, sentimental, glorified, glamorous movies. The prince on his white horse has saved his princess. A romantic fairy tale. But after a week's honeymoon she has to peel potatoes, make the bed, go to work and they'll be stuck in traffic. I wonder what their expectations are. Fairy tales or the reality of daily life? I hope they'll aim for something realistic so they won't be deceived. Tomorrow they have to proceed without party planners. I wish them well, good luck and a lot of wisdom when they return to real life.'

I ordered two glasses of champagne so we could toast to the young couple.

'May all your dreams come true,' Rachel said.

'Mazel tov,' I toasted.

'It feels good to wish two people you've never seen before well,' said Rachel. 'We just witnessed a snapshot of two peoples' lives that will stick with them forever. Maybe on an anniversary, many years from now, they'll look at the pictures or show them to their grandchildren. Or they'll fight about the photo albums during their divorce. They just said forever, but that is a dream. In the best case they'll make it happily and healthy for a long time.

One day it will end. One of them will have an affair or the contract falls apart over irreconcilable differences. Such a nice phrase for people who screwed up because they got carried away by unrealistic expectations and dreams and lack the energy to work on their relationship, be flexible, change and move forward.'

'Or one of them dies in a traffic accident,' I added. 'Just like Daisy. You are making shopping lists for the weekend, the cat on your lap, having a sip of wine and a few hours later, you spend the night in the coroner's freezer, a label on your toe.'

'That's true,' Rachel said. 'Statistically spoken chances for a divorce are fifty percent and you are right, one little mishap or cancer and the fun is done and over with. In fact, they don't really have a fair chance. Let's drink to our hopes that they belong to the minority of the real happy few.'

When we walked back to the hotel, the receptionist gave me a message from a real "happy few" couple, married for over forty years. They had lived in the United States for decades, but still had a charming Eastern-European accent. Whenever I was in town I informed them so we could share thoughts over lunch or dinner.

Harry grew up in a village in Poland. He lost his parents when he was eleven. His mother was killed by a gunshot through their kitchen door. During the invasion of Poland by the Nazis in September 1939, regular military units were accompanied by Einsatz-Gruppen. Criminals that shot Jews and others at random, looted, kicked and humiliated people. They arrested Jewish men who were severely abused in labor camps. In 1941 there already were more than two hundred such camps in Poland.

Harry told me the story shortly after we met. He was drinking a glass of milk at the kitchen table, his mother was nursing his little brother, younger by ten years. His mother was on her way to change his brother's diapers when Harry heard the sound of army boots in the street, loud laughing voices and gunshots. It all happened too fast to comprehend. His mother suddenly collapsed and dropped his baby brother on the floor. He was crying, but not badly hurt. Harry thought that his mother had fainted. He touched her face and saw blood gushing from her neck. He knew that she had been killed. In the door were two bullet holes. Although in shock, Harry did not panic. He picked up his little brother who was still crying in his dirty diapers. Harry's father had been hospitalized for an appendicitis operation. As soon as the murdering soldiers passed by, he ran to the neighbors, a family with five children. Ruth was one of them. She was his very first girlfriend. Once a week he was allowed to date her. Ruth was thirteen. They walked down to the forest and sat down on a bench in the park. She even allowed him to kiss her twice on the cheek!

Harry came gasping into his neighbor's house. Ruth's mother took care of Harry's little brother. Her father tried to comfort Harry.

'Do you want me to go to the hospital to inform your father about what happened?' he asked. 'He needs to know. I will, tomorrow,' Ruth's father promised. It was getting dark so the curfew had gone into effect; nobody was allowed to be outside. Harry stayed overnight with the neighbors.

The next morning Ruth's father went to the hospital to inform Harry's father. He stayed out for hours. Everybody became nervous as it was already getting dark. They still heard gunfire in the area. Streets were unsafe. He did not return until after dark. His wife had panicked and angrily yelled at him.

'Where have you been all this time?'

Ruth's dad did not answer his wife's question. He sat down with his coat still on and covered his face with his hands, leaning his elbows on his knees. He looked pale and was shivering. Tears were dripping from his chin onto his coat. He took a deep breath.

'They are all dead,' he whispered. 'They killed helpless, sick people. All eight of them.'

Harry was so shocked that he couldn't even react. His mother had been shot through the kitchen door in front of his eyes, his father had been killed at the hospital, while recovering from an operation? In one day his life had changed forever. No more parents to care for him and Harry realized that he couldn't take care of his little brother himself. He was alone in the world with his dependent baby brother. Ruth's parents offered to let him stay until a foster family could be found. It never happened. Hitler's troops created a trace of destruction. They forced many villagers into a wooden shack, set it on fire and then they rounded up all Jewish males to be deported to labor camps, including Harry.

Harry survived several labor and concentration camps in Poland. Towards the end of the war he, along with sixteen hundred other prisoners, were sent on a "march of death," an endless and useless ordeal. Walking from camp to camp. Prisoners were freezing to death, marching through snow and ice in sub-zero temperatures, in their worn-out concentration camp outfits. Many of them had no shoes and wrapped their feet into any piece of cloth that could be found. Often clothing from the ones that had died on the way. Many suffered from frostbite. Whoever tried to rest for a moment or slowed down was beaten or shot. Every day there were executions of sick and weak people who had no strength to go on. Or prisoners were killed without any understandable reason. Daily, at random prisoners were selected, to end up at the gallows. Others were forced to watch how they died. Who couldn't face it signed their own death sentence. They were shot on the spot. Hundreds of bodies remained behind in the snow. The survivors were forced to proceed in this madness, on their way to an unknown destruction camp, if not liberated already by the allies or destroyed by the Nazis. A prisoner's struggle to survive on the way to be killed. The ultimate cruelty. It was like the choice between dying and death.

Harry and fifty others were forced at gunpoint to cross the Russian front, yet another terrifying experience. Heavy, bloody fighting was going on between Russian and German troops, the latter were losing rapidly. Harry was sure that they didn't stand a chance to survive. It looked like a suicide mission. Shots were fired all over, occasionally a grenade landed close to them, two of them stepped on a landmine. They were surrounded by soldiers mutilated beyond recognition, wounded, in pain, screaming for help. Harry's group was unable to help them or members of their own who were wounded. Often shredded to pieces they had to be left behind until their bodies gave in to frostbite or their injuries.

Suddenly they came face to face with Russian soldiers. Initially they were threatened and intimidated. They were all forced at gunpoint, to lay face down in the snow for hours, their hands on their heads. After that they received a fairly decent reception. Soldiers took them to a military camp, gave them warm clothes, shoes and food. Harry was taken to a field hospital where he was treated for frostbite. He lost three toes. At the hospital he made plans to join the Russian forces to fight the Nazis. These plans and his original dream to be liberated by the Russians did not come true. Without reason he was arrested by the military police and deported to Siberia. Once again he had become a slave-laborer, isolated from the rest of the world. He wasn't even told when the war ended.

In 1947 he was released without explanation. He returned to the village where he grew up. He didn't recognize anything nor anyone. Not one living soul was able or willing to tell him what had happened to his little brother and to Ruth, her parents, brothers and sisters. Houses had been destroyed or were occupied by strangers. They made it clear that he was not welcome in the village anymore.

Homeless and broke he finally found himself a job on a foreign cargo ship. After seven years working below deck, in the noise and fumes of the engine room, the ship moored in San Pedro, near Los Angeles. He decided to walk off the ship. He had saved a little money, enough to survive for a few months.

After tiresome correspondence with bureaucracies in Europe, he discovered that there was one surviving family member. His father's nephew had fled in 1937 and was now running an ophthalmologist's practice in a suburb of London. Every month he sent Harry some money and paid the prohibitive attorney fees for Harry's legal immigration.

Harry's old girlfriend Ruth had left the Polish village days after the men had been deported. A friendly German soldier had warned her that there were plans to execute the entire population. He offered her a ride to a neighboring town on his motorbike and gave her all his money.

'Dead soldiers don't need money,' he told Ruth.

It did not take her far, without a proper ID. She was arrested at the railroad station when she tried to board a train. She spent months in several camps.

Most names she could not recall.

'They didn't take us there by taxi,' she once said. 'The final destination was where the train coincidentally stopped.'

After one of these transports she felt that she would not survive without a miracle.

'The smell of death was all over the place,' she told me. 'In the dark we noticed the chimneys of the crematoria spitting fire and ashes into the cold skies.'

The newly arrived prisoners stood in line for hours. officers and camp doctors judged who would live and who wouldn't. An SS officer walked by the prisoners.

'What are your skills?' he asked Ruth.

'I am a professional pianist,' she made up on the spot.

The officer took Ruth by the shoulder and pushed her to the line of those who would live for a while. At least a delay of execution.

Ruth had played the piano since early childhood. She followed lessons, was extremely talented but had never performed in public.

The first days in the camp were an ordeal. In the freezing cold, dressed in their camp outfits they were endlessly drilled.

A week later the SS officer picked her up during one of these drills in front of her barrack. He took her to an officers' mess with a piano.

He seemed like a reasonable person to her.

'Play something,' he ordered her.

Ruth started to shake all over, fearing it would be discovered that she had lied. That would mean the end.

The officer kindly took her shaking hand.

'Relax, don't be afraid,' he said. 'My name is Dieter. You don't have to be scared of me. I didn't invent all this hypocrisy. Just play me something pretty. We can use some happiness in the midst of all of this madness.'

Ruth played a nocturne by Chopin, the only piece she knew perfectly well. Dieter listened carefully, leaning back in a lounge chair, smoking a cigarette. He did not touch the glass of *schnapps* he had poured himself. He interrupted Ruth's performance abruptly by applauding loudly.

'This is excellent,' he praised her. 'You have great talent. You are going to be a famous performer.'

From that moment Ruth received a little better treatment. Each day she was allowed to rehearse on the piano in the officers' mess, was dispensed of hard labor and received some acceptable food.

Each weekend she had to perform during parties, at the German side of the camp, away from the barracks, torture, illnesses and the crematoria, puking ashes. It was disgusting to her, seeing the officers gourmandize and getting drunk in the midst of the destruction. The officers loved her music. Ruth tried to study their faces while she was playing. Faces of sadists and mass murderers. She shut herself off from reality, put her mind in another world. She fantasized about playing on the stage of a glorious concert hall, performing with the national symphony orchestra, wearing a beautiful long black silk gala dress.

Several times she was taken to an establishment in a nearby village. A hangout only for the highest officers, all of them heavily intoxicated and enjoying a large number of local hookers, whose businesses were booming. SS officers, half undressed stumbled down the stairs, lipstick all over their necks and shoulders. Dieter was there too. Apparently he had fun, pretending to play the flute with Ruth, using a metal pipe. Bystanders were cheering and clapping their hands encouraging him to go on. Suddenly his mood changed. He hit Ruth on both hands with the metal pipe, breaking seven of her fingers.

'Stop this fucking, Jewish music,' he yelled at her. 'I'll smash all of your fingers. You don't need them anyhow in the gas chamber.' He staggered a few steps and then collapsed. Ruth was still sitting at the piano, in severe pain, her eyes closed, biting her tongue to avoid screaming out loud. As she felt a hand on her shoulder she winced out of fear. It was one of the hookers.

'We have to get you out of here, child,' she whispered. 'If you don't, these scumbags are going to kill you.'

She instructed some of the other women to use every bit of their professional charms to keep the drunken officers busy.

She waited until she was sure that no one was paying attention to them.

'Now,' she hissed into Ruth's ear and pushed her to an exit.

The hooker covered Ruth with her coat and took her home.

She treated Ruth's broken fingers as best as she could. She could not call a doctor, fearing they would be betrayed to the Nazis. The woman took good care of Ruth. She fed her well, altered some of her warm clothes so Ruth could wear them, gave her one of her wigs, making her look like an attractive adult. Spending a fortune on corrupt German authorities she obtained relatively secure travel documents.

Ruth walked and hitchhiked through Germany, Holland, Belgium, France, across the Pyrenees mountains, via the Spanish border, into Portugal.

When I asked her how long that took, she answered, 'Too many lifetimes. It would take me a lifetime to tell you about the arrests, the escapes, passing front lines. In France I was released from a concentration camp thanks to a wealthy family who paid the Nazis large sums of money to let a few young people go. They needed one more person. That was me. A miracle. I escaped to the United States via Portugal, which was a miracle too. Portugal had closed its borders to refugees in May of 1940. There was a small group of influential, rich business people who helped refugees. They bribed both the Portuguese and American immigration. Just prior to me boarding the ship to the United States, I learned about a Portuguese man who individually saved thousands of lives.'

In 1940 tens of thousands of refugees were on the run from Hitler's advancing troops. Portuguese diplomats had received an order not to issue any more visas. One of these diplomats, Sousa Mendes, the Portuguese Consul General in Bordeaux, disobeyed the new order. He was sanctioned and recalled to Lisbon to be disciplined. The Consulate General was bombed by the Germans. On his way home, he stopped at the diplomatic mission in Bayonne, near the French-Spanish border. There he ordered thousands of visas to be issued, providing the refugees with safe passage through Spain and entrance to Portugal. He alone, with some help of a colleague in Toulouse, saved an estimated ten thousand people, or more. When Sousa Mendes returned to Lisbon he was disciplined, received practically no salary or benefits. He became an outcast. There was also an unofficial punishment. The blacklisting and social banishment of Aristides de

Sousa Mendes and his family who were forced to take meals at the soup kitchen of the Jewish community of Lisbon. He lived the rest of his years in deep poverty until his death in 1954, owing money to many lenders and still in disgrace with his government. But he had no regrets, acting as a good Catholic. During his life he never received recognition for his heroic actions.

Ruth arrived in New York in late 1943. Her Portuguese rescuers had made arrangements with a foster family in Los Angeles. She went to college and university, earning a master's degree in psychology.

After the end of the war she started checking International Red Cross lists to see if anyone of her family had survived. None of them had. She also checked out the fate of her former neighbors. They were all listed dead, except for Harry. He was unaccounted for. She had remembered Harry telling her about a relative who had fled to England. Via the British consulate she obtained a list of persons with Harry's last name, an irregular, Polish name. She wrote to them all, asking for possible information on Harry's whereabouts. Most of them wrote her a short note, telling her that they were not related to Harry. Her last hopes vanished. She felt brokenhearted. Ruth was left alone with a good job, an outstanding education but feeling extremely lonely and depressed. In the fall of 1954 she received a letter from London, from Harry's relative. He wrote that he had received her letter, had saved it because he himself was searching for survivors. He gave her Harry's address, ironically enough not even half an hour away from where she lived. Three months later they got married and moved to San Diego.

Ruth built her own private practice and Harry, who had no education, started an appliance store with financial support from his English relative. Both men were devoted and enjoyed running the business.

Ten years later they owned a chain of over twenty stores, selling tools, household appliances and later sophisticated electronics. They sold their company in 1988 and retired. Harry and Ruth bought a cozy villa in La Jolla, overlooking the Pacific Ocean.

'Now we only see beauty, every morning as we wake up,' Ruth repeatedly said.

When I called Harry from the hotel he invited Rachel and me to dinner.

'We celebrate another anniversary today,' he said. 'I lost track. I don't know which one. Forty-something. It's been a lifetime. Nice to have good company at our celebration. Ruth and I will pick you up at eight from your hotel.'

'Mazel tov,' I said.

'Oy,' he answered. 'Getting old is no accomplishment. Maybe getting old together is? It simply happens when you don't argue too much and you don't die.'

At eight o'clock sharp Ruth and Harry walked into the lobby of the hotel. Ruth looked as if she had stopped aging in her mid forties, a pretty, young woman, in one of her gorgeous outfits. During the war, in one of the camps, she had promised herself that if she would survive, be free, have money, she would dress up every day like a lady. She had kept that promise. Ruth wore beautiful clothes each day, even when she didn't go out.

I introduced Rachel to them. We all kissed.

'I made a reservation down the street,' Harry said. 'Let's walk.'

We started to stroll down the pretty main street. Ruth and Rachel stopped at a store. Harry and I sat down on a bench. He started to comment on a movie on the Holocaust, he had just seen.

'It was well made,' he said. 'But it was strange, unrealistic. Parts were just made up. Most of the people in the theater were crying but I was wondering why? Crying about what? An expensive Hollywood production, created by well known expensive writers, directors and actors. Of course the budget for such a film doesn't nearly reach the level of what the Nazis and the so called civilized world have stolen from us. Money can do miracles, but you can't buy real emotions. This was so remote from what Ruth and I went through. In a movie stories make sense. You get a look behind the scenes where the Nazis worked on their plans, the victims, heroes and with every person you see the beginning, middle and end of each individual story. That's not the way it was. One of the worst terrors was isolation. You had no clue as to what was going to happen the next minute. In the barrack next to yours, at the Officers' Mess where it was decided if you would live or die. You had absolutely no idea what was happening in the world. You lived from coincidence to coincidence, each time miraculously escaping death. It was an enormous feeling of loneliness, being the forgotten outcasts of the world. We reached a point that we wondered why the allied airplanes didn't bomb the concentration camps. People cry, watching fabricated Hollywood productions full of ridiculous fiction, but they didn't seem to mind when it was really happening and we were tortured and gassed. They closed their borders on us. They didn't cry when Idi Amin committed genocide in Uganda, not a tear about Rwanda or the bloodshed in former Yugoslavia, which we followed on television. When cruelty is far away life goes on, when it comes close it becomes scary. Terrorism was not our problem until 9/11. When people ask me to tell something about the war, I feel that they shut themselves off. I am coming too close. Maybe they think it's babbling, whining by an old man. Perhaps a movie is an ideal solution. It's on the silver screen, you can cry anonymously in the dark and you know that by the time the lights come on, the story has come to a good end. Time for a second showing of fiction. Our truth may become fiction at the end, to new generations.

For us it is still for real. First the war, then for me the cold shower right after and now, while getting older we relive it once more. Not to mention the poor, the ones that never lucked out and struggle every day in poverty. But maybe I am just a grumpy, jealous old man. I wish that I could have been one of these famous actors, comfortably relaxing in a luxurious trailer. Knock, knock on your door. You go to the make-up and on to the set. The director yells, "Birkenau, gas chamber, take twenty." You say your lines, work a few months earning several millions in Auschwitz-Birkenau, enjoy the best catering at the Birkenau set and return to Beverly Hills. You read in the papers that millions of people are crying, watching you in movie theaters. No one watched when it happened in reality.

"Let go of the past, you wealthy, old man," people say. Maybe they're right. Sometimes it's difficult to understand people.'

Ruth and Rachel came out of the store. Ruth had treated herself to a new dress and had bought Rachel a small, elegant purse.

'Pretty people deserve pretty things,' Ruth said.

'Ugly people too,' Harry responded, pointing first at himself and then to me.

As we continued to walk he whispered to me, 'Your taste is not bad. That is an endearing, beautiful woman. Not a bad philosophy, you have. Being alone is no fun and when you decide to attract company you are better off by a young pretty woman like her than an old whiner like me.'

At the restaurant I ordered a bottle of champagne to toast to their anniversary. Ruth showed us some pictures of a recent trip to South Africa. It was the fulfillment of another wish she made during the years of persecution. To travel the world. Ruth went on a big trip, twice a year.

After his retirement Harry joined her once a year.

'Why sit in an airplane for twenty hours when I have the nicest view in the world from my back yard? If I want to see a zebra I drive to the San Diego Wild Life Park, if I want to communicate with different races and cultures I walk around the block.'

'Next year we go to Indonesia,' Ruth told us. 'Seven weeks, from island to island.'

While she said this Harry took a little gift box out of his pocket. A present for Ruth.

'Here,' he interrupted her. 'A medal of honor and appreciation for another year of reasonable treatment.'

It was an antique, gold European coin on a necklace.

They both got up and kissed for almost a full minute. The waiter took Polaroid pictures and gave them to us. Harry and Ruth hugging and kissing like a young couple in love, Rachel with a shy smile, me smiling at the kissing couple.

'Isn't it funny? We are still in love after all these years,' Ruth said, smiling.

She picked up her knife and fork with her damaged fingers. Broken by Dieter, the drunken SS officer who had saved her life.

Ruth and Harry both were marked for life, but still able to enjoy.

After dinner Ruth wanted to take a walk. I decided to join her. Harry and Rachel went to the hotel for an after dinner drink. Ruth and I walked down to the park, sat down on a bench enjoying the smells and sounds of the ocean in the dark.

I knew that Ruth was waiting for the right moment to ask a few personal questions.

'Are Rachel and you...' she started.

I interrupted her.

'No, we are not going to get married. We are old friends. To be specific, we are lovers but we won't stay together.'

'Why not?' Ruth asked. 'She is a very remarkable woman. Intelligent, loving, fun, pretty too. What else do you want?'

'And much more than that,' I replied. 'She is like family, like a sister, a *Partner in Crime*, sometimes even like a mother.'

'Then marry her,' said Ruth.

'I don't think so,' I responded. 'Rachel is part of my past and present. In fact, Daisy gave me everything that I missed out on during childhood. That was heavenly, but when she died I stood empty handed. I lost it all in one split second. I'll either stay alone or I'll share my life with someone who is not connected to the past. A friend of mine recently said that nobody is irreplaceable. That may be true but every individual is unique. I am not scared to face a future without a partner, without planning, full of uncertainties. Life goes on.'

'Perhaps you are right,' Ruth responded. 'In fact Harry has always replaced the people that I've lost. That miraculously worked. I am also mothering him a little bit. I never gave it a thought, but he wouldn't be replaceable. In business you can replace a president, in politics a conservative for a liberal liar and vice versa, but not in your personal life. But Rachel is exceptional and irreplaceable too.'

'We would start off with unrealistic expectations,' I answered. 'I am still at the stage that I want to replace Daisy. It takes time to get over that. Having Rachel take her place wouldn't be fair, because it's not what she needs and not what I want. We love each other but right now we both have unrealistic expectations. That wouldn't be a healthy start.'

'That's why most marriages don't work,' said Ruth. 'People usually have a long, ambitious list of expectations. A sort of hidden agenda, because they rarely tell each other openly what it is they want. Perhaps they don't even know. Most people don't even share their sexual fantasies or how they want to be pleased in bed. Very strange. They share their lives, houses, money but not their real feelings. In marriage counseling I listen to one, then to the other, often they both sound reasonable but every time I think, are these people talking about the same issues? Are they really living under one roof? Two totally different stories about their mutual lives. Most of the time because they are disappointed in each other, the other doesn't perform according to their expectations. Seldom can people let go of them, change, develop, be creative. They stand still, they become frustrated, angry, unhappy. Both trying to manipulate the other into the direction that they have in mind. They mostly refuse to discuss what they really feel and expect.'

'Daisy and I simply didn't have too many expectations,' I said. 'We took things as they were. We didn't make too many plans either. If you make too many plans you need to keep changing them. You can't always expect to understand each other. Even though we shared most thoughts, I was never really able to explain how it was to grow up with my parents, in an Amsterdam neighborhood, just after the war. A world completely apart from her relatively happy childhood in Los Angeles. She somehow had a good rapport with the *Partners in Crime*, became one of them, but that was more out of mutual affection than understanding. And a lack of expectation to be understood. That isn't always necessary. But most people want to be understood.'

'Harry and I never had children for that reason,' Ruth said. 'We would have expected them to understand us, what happened to us.

That would have been unfair and impossible. Yet we would have been disappointed. And God knows what they would have expected from us? Our relationship is fragile enough, but somehow we manage to provide for one another. That by itself is an exceptional blessing. I might have given birth to a *Partner in Crime*.'

'What do you mean?' I asked.

'Another child from emotionally damaged parents,' she answered. 'Let me be clear. After the war all of us were eager to pick up the remaining pieces of life and start over again. We wanted to create new families. A natural desire. But were we fit to manage a family? I doubt it. And, as you said, one should not try to attempt to replace the deceased but carry on. Most of the children of Holocaust survivors collapse at some point. Mostly at age forty or fifty, when life starts taking its toll and they feel that they are no longer in control. Pleasing their demanding parents failed. They were unrealistically expected to perform, be successful. They had to hide their feelings. They had to make up for the lost ones, careers have their ups and downs, good health is not a given fact, marriages drain energy. Most of them have been burning the candle from both ends in a struggle to survive. The Holocaust did not come to an end in 1945, we all know that. After such a disaster many generations suffer to a certain extent. You are right that expectations can be destructive. People want something without realizing it, due to their background. One of my patients - a child-survivor - always goes to hookers. Every relationship he blew because of that desire. As a child he had been hidden for several years by a hooker. Of course he started to have sexual fantasies as a young boy. But he could only relate them to the professional skills of his rescuer. It turned him on and it still does. He divorced twice, has three children, lives in poverty because of the large sum of monthly child support. A hopeless case. Sad and lonely.'

'Why don't you advise him to marry a hooker?' I suggested with a smile.

'Maybe that's a good idea,' Ruth responded. 'That will lead to another divorce. You know what always stuns me? That even after a marriage breaks up both parties still do anything to attract each other's attention. They argue about money and the children. Strangely enough women automatically take for granted that a man is unable to raise children, so the mother fights for custody. Then they start to complain about the low amount of child support they receive, the hardship of being a single mother and deny the kids to see their dads. Don't I have a wonderful profession?'

'Let's go join Harry and Rachel,' I suggested.

We walked back to the hotel.

'How are your parents?' Ruth asked.

'So-so,' I answered. 'My father hasn't been well for a while and I am concerned about what will happen to my mother if he dies.'

'Maybe I shouldn't say this,' Ruth responded. 'She may be more egocentric than you think. It wouldn't surprise me at all if she will experience his death as a relief and start all over for herself.'

'I doubt if you are right this time,' I said. 'Anyhow, thanks for your complementary professional advice.'

'Every time we talk I wonder, am I walking the dog or is it the other way around,' she responded.

When Harry and Ruth left, Ruth kissed Rachel and gave her an open invitation.

'Come see us again, sweetie. If you ever want to stay with us, just let me know.'

Rachel and I went up to our room.

'What darling people they are,' Rachel said. 'They just feel like family to me. But so do you.'

We kissed goodnight.

The next morning we drove north, direction Los Angeles on the secondary coastal road. A pretty ride. We took a walk along the ocean on Seal Beach, spent a couple of hours at an outside terrace in the Marina del Rey, overlooking the yacht harbor. At eight o'clock we arrived at Café Montmartre in Santa Monica, to have dinner and see Pierre. He had decorated the place with Christmas lights and a chanukiah.

Pierre hugged me, took Rachel by the arm to my regular table were Pierre had already opened a bottle of my favorite wine.

'Your brother called,' he said to me. 'If you need some privacy, feel free to use my office. Take your time. I'll bore this beautiful lady to tears with a few old jokes.'

I went into Pierre's office to call Eric.

'I got your postcard,' he said. 'I've been thinking about it too. How is he?'

'Not good. I called yesterday,' I answered. 'He finally underwent a complete physical. They have to wait for the lab reports and test results, but it doesn't look good. His condition weakens every day.'

'Let me go to another phone,' he said.

He put me on hold for several minutes.

'I have been thinking but I haven't discussed it with Irene,' he explained. 'In fact, it's none of her business and in this case I can't have her judgmental remarks. Just for the sake of myself I'd like you to keep me informed on what's going on. If there is a real chance that he is going to die in the foreseeable future, I want to make arrangements so that at least I can be there and be assured that he rests in peace.'

'I'll let you know as soon as I hear something,' I promised. 'I'm proud of you that you have made your own, personal decision. You have to live with it, the rest of your life, not Irene.'

When I came back to my table Pierre excused himself. A large group of people had come in for a birthday dinner.

'Come back tomorrow night so we can have dinner together and chat a little bit,' he said.

'I will.' I promised.

During our dinner I was thinking about my phone conversation with Eric. Perhaps there finally was going to be one occasion that the family could be united in peace?

Rachel interrupted my thoughts.

'I've had an unforgettable time with you,' she said. 'Too bad that I have to go home tomorrow, but time is up and duty is calling. Back to home and back to work. You behave yourself while I'm gone. In just a few weeks we'll be reunited. I talked to Dave this morning. He said that everything has been arranged, flight reservations, hotel rooms and so on.'

'So everyone is still serious?' I asked.

'Sure,' Rachel answered. 'Everyone has his self interested motives. Dave will even cut a business trip short. When are you planning on coming?'

'In about a week,' I answered. 'Tomorrow afternoon I have an appointment in this area, then I want to relax and be on my own for a few days.'

'Have I been draining you?' Rachel asked.

'On the contrary,' I answered. 'I enjoyed every minute of your company and I will miss you. I just want to be prepared for the trip. I have to go back into my home again, prepare for the exceptional reunion of the *Partners in Crime* and I have to visit my parents. Maybe see my father for the last time. It's not going to be easy.'

'I'm afraid you are right,' Rachel said. 'Let's go to the hotel so we have a long last night together.'

The next morning I called Dave who told me all the details about the arrangements he had made, where and when we would meet.

'We have a minyan,' he proudly announced. 'They are all coming. Boy called me. He and Molly will be there too.'

In the afternoon I took Rachel to the airport, all the way to the "passengers only" sign. We kissed goodbye for minutes.

'Take good care. We'll meet again at the cemetery,' I said.

She waved and smiled until she was through the security check and was out of sight. I was struggling to control my tears. The moment she started to walk away from me I already missed her and felt lonely. I looked at my watch and realized that I had to hurry for my appointment with Horst Sachsse,* the man who had known my uncle Sammy before he was arrested at his hiding place and killed by the Nazis.

* See page 34.

22

A week later I flew from Los Angeles to Amsterdam. My mother had told me that the results of the medical tests had confirmed what we feared. My father had terminal cancer.

I asked her how much longer he had.

'They don't know,' she answered emotionally . 'It may be a matter of days.'

I called Eric to tell him the bad news. He canceled all his appointments and prepared for a rapid departure. He was in a terrible fight with his wife.

She found it ridiculous that he would travel across the Atlantic to attend the funeral of his father, who had kicked him out of the house at age eight and after that had never supported him in any way. As we were talking on the phone she was still yelling at him.

'It is very difficult for me now,' he said. 'But this time I'll do what I want.'

I went straight from Amsterdam airport to my parents' house, suffering from jet lag after a thirteen-hour flight.

My mother opened the front door.

'Are you walking around without a scarf in the middle of winter?' she reprimanded me.

Then she started to whisper.

'Your father is very sick now. The cancer has spread throughout his body, from the colon to the liver. The doctor says that he may die any moment. He sleeps most of the time.'

We walked into the living room.

'Can I get you some tea?' she asked me.

I said yes. While she was fixing tea in the kitchen I tried to think what to do. Maybe I should stay around and support my mother for a while? The idea didn't attract me. As the oldest son I should be at the funeral and say Kaddish at my father's grave.

My mother walked into the room, carrying a tray with a pot of tea, two cups and big chunks of apple pie and whipped cream.

'He is dying because of his own conceitedness,' she said. 'It made him survive the war, successful in life, now it kills him. When he became ill he refused to have his intestines examined. But what shall I say? He is eighty-seven. A person needs to die of something.'

She poured two cups of tea and served her homemade apple pie. Apparently her bakery was still in full swing.

'How is he emotionally coping with it?' I asked.

'What shall I say? It's becoming worse each day. It's just like a candle, you watch him burn to the end. There is not much left. Sometimes he doesn't even recognize me anymore. Or he pretends, I don't know.'

In between the talking she wolfed down her apple pie.

'What are you going to do?' I asked. 'Have you given that any thought? If you want me to, I can stay with you for a while.'

'Thank you, that won't be necessary,' she replied. 'The day he dies I am out of here. I'll be with him as long as I can handle him, but everything must come to an end. Years ago I bought myself into a luxurious nursing home in Israel. Your father didn't know. I thought, if one of us will be alone one day, we don't have any friends or relatives here, so why not enjoy the last years in a good climate? During the past few weeks I arranged for the move and the sale of the house. A realtor I know will take care of that. When you want to sell your house at a good price, one should not be in a hurry, you know? I'll sell most of the household effects. I am not going to move all that old furniture and your dad's immense library.'

I was flabbergasted about this harsh business-like approach. While my father was dying she had been planning her new future.

'How about the funeral ceremony?' I asked.

'There isn't going to be one,' she answered. 'He will be buried in silence and that's all. No one would attend the funeral service anyhow. We don't have any friends or family. Maybe you and I. We wouldn't even have a minyan. Eric won't come, the grandchildren don't even know him. Maybe the doctor, out of politeness.'

She poured herself some more tea and started to swallow another piece of apple pie.

'I believe that you need to discuss it with Eric too,' I said. 'Maybe he wants to attend. You need to give him a chance to say farewell to his father. It's his choice.'

'No, it is not,' my mother said determinedly. 'Eric caused us a lot of grief. We never heard from him when your father was healthy, so why now all of a sudden? Your father wouldn't want that anyhow.'

'Can I talk to him for a moment?' I asked.

'Let me take a look if he is awake,' she answered.

I listened to her heavy footsteps in the hallway. The same footsteps that scared me so many times when I was a child. I wanted to talk to my father. Passing away in peace is a human right.

'You may come,' my mother yelled through the house.

I walked to their bedroom. He was lying on top of his blankets, only wearing a robe. He looked skinny like a concentration camp prisoner, was unshaven, quivering against a pillow.

'How do you feel?'

He did not respond.

'Do you want to talk to me?' I tried again.

He kept staring vacuously forward.

'Would you like me to stay with you? Keeping you company?'

Suddenly he turned his head, looked me straight into the eyes with a reprehensible expression of anger and hate. Just for a couple of seconds. Then he locked me out forever by closing his eyes on me.

'He remains difficult all the way to the end,' my mother said as we walked back into the living room. 'He always lived in a small world, now there is hardly something left. He loves you, but actually didn't want to see you,' she explained. 'I am the only one he allows to take care of him. Your father is a very bitter man. He talked about the grandchildren. Not about Eric. He will die a lonely man, a situation that he created himself. No one was good enough for him, he didn't trust anyone, was not particularly friendly to others. Now he doesn't want to live anymore. That's up to him. Meanwhile I am working on my departure. Maybe I can enjoy a few years without too many worries. That's up to me. I respected him but I had my share. I did the best I could, had to tolerate a lot. He always needed me, now I need myself.'

'Do you need me to help you pack?' I asked.

'No, thanks again. His valuables I will sell, the other things go to the WIZO. The rest I'll trash. So there really isn't too much to pack and I am better off without you around. Too many chefs in the kitchen.'

'Don't you care about what I want?' I asked.

'I am your mother, I know how you feel. You are my own flesh and blood so you don't need to tell me. I know.'

She started to cry.

'That worthless brother of yours. I gave birth to him and he doesn't even talk to his own mother.'

She moaned and complained about Eric for about twenty minutes.

'If you haven't talked to him for such a long time, why are you whining at me?' I asked. 'Call him if you wish to communicate.'

My mother jumped up and started to yell. 'Is that the way you talk to your mother? You think that you can give orders to me, you idiot? Did you come to ridicule me while your father is suffering and dying, during my weakest point of sadness? Don't you respect your parents at all?'

She walked in my direction, screaming in Yiddish and tried to slap me in the face. I grabbed her wrist, right in time.

'The beatings belong to the past,' I said. 'Everything comes to an end, you just said.'

She started to laugh through her tears.

'Are you staying for dinner?' she asked. 'I've made wonderful soup and your father doesn't eat anymore. It would be a shame if it would go to waste. Do you know how much they charge for soup meat nowadays? I'd rather have you eat it than trash it later. I am not eating any of it because I am on a diet. Can you tell? I've already lost four and a half pounds in two weeks. Must be anxiety about your father too.'

I wrote a phone number down for her.

'Here is a number where you can reach me for the next few days if you need me or change your mind about the funeral. If not, I wish you well in Israel.'

I got up and walked to the front door.

My mother disappeared into the kitchen and returned with two plastic containers from her refrigerator, filled with soup.

'Here,' she babbled. 'Home made as usual. Maybe you should eat some later, in your hotel. That's healthier than the junk they dare to serve you at their restaurant. Just tell someone in the kitchen to heat it up for you in the microwave for about two minutes, if they don't find that too much to ask. Perhaps they'll even provide you with a spoon, for all that money that you are spending there.'

She grabbed one of my father's wool scarves and put it tight around my neck.

'You have to dress warm in this freezing cold,' she said. 'Your father won't wear it anymore so you may keep it, but I need the plastic containers. I use them a lot and they don't sell the same brand anymore. They are very practical and part of a set, you see.'

I kissed her goodbye.

'Don't forget to eat the soup,' she yelled as I walked to the car. 'It contains a lot of vitamin C. You need that in winter or you'll catch the flu.'

She closed the front door.

With my hand, I wiped snow from the windshield. I poured the soup in a bush, put the empty containers underneath their mailbox.

'Goodbye house where I was born, goodbye parents,' I whispered as I drove away.

"It contains a lot of vitamin C, you need that in winter or you'll catch the flu," had been her last words to me. My father's last words I couldn't exactly recall. Maybe they referred to my deceased uncle: "You look a lot like him but you are not as intelligent," or something to that extent. In New York he had refused to come out of a bathroom to say goodbye. Maybe he just had a hard time parting?

He died the next day, at four o'clock in the afternoon. At his request a doctor helped him out of his misery. Shortly afterwards my mother moved to a nursing home in Israel. She passed away before I had a chance to visit her. My father's scarf I left in the rental car.

23

The day before my *Partners in Crime* arrived I got organized. A meeting with my accountant who had to take care of my tax return, a brief session with Ron and the finalizing of the paperwork at an attorney's office for Ron to buy me out.

After that I had a very pleasant lunch with Ron and Meta.

'We miss you a lot,' she stated several times.

She gave me the envelope from the police department with Daisy's belongings after she died, that I had never opened. A small purse, her silk scarf, credit cards, a driver's license, a lipstick, money, the necklace and bracelet made out of golden daisies that I gave her as a wedding gift on the roof terrace of Dick and Beverly's penthouse in San Francisco, her wedding ring, a picture of her and me at the Catalina Island heliport and a small gift wrapped photo album. A surprise for me. On page one she had put a photograph of herself hugging the cat with handwritten text: "I'm never going to let go of you."

In the hotel room that Dave had arranged for, I took ample time inserting the pictures that I had collected over the past twelve months. Ted and Rivka, drinking coffee at my house during the shiva, Dave, Leslie and me in a restaurant in San Francisco, Pierre in front of Café Montmartre in Santa Monica, the group picture of the *Partners in Crime*; Fred, Michael, Sally, Phil and Joan, Esther, Mony, Rachel, Max and Gaby, Dave and Leslie, David and me in a New York hotel, snapshots of Suzy and her "China man," Boy and Molly, Eric and me in front of a New York theater, Harry and Ruth kissing in a restaurant in La Jolla, Horst Sachsse and his wife Ursula in front of their big Christmas tree, overloaded with ornaments. Pages of endearing memories and touching moments.

Rachel came to my room early in the afternoon prior to December fifteenth.

'You're still all over me,' she said. 'Can we lie down and hug before the others arrive?'

We did, for almost half an hour, quietly. Me lying on my back, Rachel sideways with her head on my chest. It was like an unorchestrated meditation. Two people creating an oasis of peace, sheltering from the world, sharing the same thoughts and feelings. At five-thirty Dave and Leslie, Michael, Esther and Sally arrived, squeezed like sardines into a small European car. Shortly afterwards Mony, Phil and Joan, Max and David. Fred was the last to arrive.

'I'm sorry about your dad,' Fred said. 'My condolences. Strange how it all happened. I tried to call your mother but she had already left, I guess. The phone was disconnected.'

'It was a bizarre, last chapter of his history,' I responded. 'But that's the way it was.'

'How did your brother react to it?' asked Sally.

'I informed him on each and every development,' I answered. 'He had already decided to come to the funeral. When I told him that neither of us had been invited, his world collapsed. He was furious and in tears on the phone. And you know what? Irene, who always became furious when Eric talked about my parents, surprised both of us. Maybe my judgment of her was unsubstantiated. When she heard Eric cry, she picked up another phone and said, "This is the ultimate selfish act of family terrorism. It's up to Eric what he wants to do and how he needs to say farewell to his deceased father. He shall not be manipulated."

Both of them are here. They arrived early this morning from New York. They are taking a nap now, until dinner.'

'Are they joining us?' Mony asked.

'They are,' I confirmed.

'Just a question of order,' Sally said to Dave. 'When you need to buy new cigars on the corner of the street, you order one of these tasteless, huge limos. So how come today you squeezed the five of us in a little rental?'

'There are no more limos in my life,' Dave answered. 'No more limos and no more hotel suites. Lately I have been staying at regular hotel rooms, just like the rabble. I discussed all of these habits with my psychiatrist. He charges a fortune, but by telling me to skip some of my habits he saves me a fortune. So in fact I'm making a profit on the quack.'

'Somehow I am under the impression that you didn't fly tourist class out here,' Esther said. 'And what about the fancy restaurants?'

'Oh well, you can't win them all at the same time,' Dave replied. 'Therapy takes time, step by step. I am a patient now. That word originated in French, *patience*. That means that people should have some patience with me.'

'I always thought that the patient needed to be patient,' Rachel said.

'Usually yes,' Dave answered. 'Not in my case. I am an exception. I am different. I am intelligent, gifted, charming and modest. Since I have these exceptional skills, I proclaim myself as leader, call me

President, no, Führer of this obscure group. I have a proposal, no, an order.'

'Your wish is my Befehl, Oberst-Gruppenführer,' Michael responded and saluted, clearly showing a lack of military skills.

'Call that brother of yours and tell him and Irene to come down here,' Dave said to me.

Five minutes later Eric and Irene walked into the room.

'I had been planning to invite you all to dinner tomorrow,' Dave declaimed. 'But on second thought I think it's better that we go our own way after the Kaddish. We all came here with our own individual inducements, thoughts and emotions. Not as a team. It would not be appropriate if we would go out, immediately afterwards and throw one of our famous, destructive parties. That would take us back to where we started. Like at the Habonim camps and our farewell breakfast in New York. After tomorrow we'll all leave with our personal thoughts and go on with our lives. After going back to the past I believe we should all go home, into the future.'

'That sounds thoughtful to me,' Sally said.

'I knew you would agree,' Dave continued. 'However, I am not going to deny my *Partners in Crime* an exquisite dinner. That wouldn't be fair. So instead I'll take you out tonight. In a couple of hours. Reservations have been made so we don't need a democratic, time-consuming discussion on this issue. I suggest that we use the remaining time, before we go out, telling each other what we will be thinking about tomorrow during the Kaddish. That way we'll be able to share our emotions. We are privileged because we are in a position that we can comfortably do so. We are here because we want to, or need to be. Not to meet anyone's expectations. The clubhouse gave us more than a safe shelter. It gave us the opportunity to be ourselves.

A place where we could ask for healthy attention, comforted each other. We could not do that at home. There we had to pay attention and be on the alert. Together we had the opportunity to test our behavior, borders if you will, have fun and show anger, frustrations without repercussions. That's how we more or less learned to set our boundaries of normal, human behavior. We were unable to do that at home. It would have confused our parents and damaged their expectations. The emotional balance was too fragile. Tomorrow you are free to experience, do and think whatever you wish. You won't harm anyone. We have granted ourselves that permission a few weeks ago, after David's Bar Mitzvah. We deserve that. We are not only around to please others. We learned that from friends, spouses, as adults, not when we were children as it is supposed to be. But, better late than never. Now let's talk so we can go out to dinner and return to our usual, reckless and decadent behavior.'

'You are a treasure,' Sally told Dave. 'To make it easy on you. I'll begin.'

The remaining two hours until dinner we spent quietly listening to each other. When we walked into the restaurant Boy and Molly were waiting for us.

24

The next day all *Partners in Crime* stood in a circle around Daisy's grave.

The rabbi greeted me with a friendly smile.

'I don't really know what you guys are up to, but I am glad that at least we have a minyan,' he said.

Everyone was dressed in warm winter clothes. There was a chilling wind and it had just started snowing.

'You don't need my explanation as to why we are together here today,' the rabbi spoke while snowflakes landed on his hat and black coat.

'Jewish law tells us exactly what the procedures for mourning are. Of course we respect the laws to the letter, but as individuals we also live according to the spirit of the law. Each individual, with the help of the Almighty, needs to find a way to determine how to deal with losing a beloved one. We can find strength through belief and our traditions. That's why we never are alone. We have the Almighty and each other. Together we must find a way to carry on, preserve our high values, be good to the ones we love, come to terms with reality, even if that is harsh and cruel. Only then can we come to terms with sadness and preserve faith that life is worthwhile.'

While the rabbi continued I looked around. A chain of people, circled around Daisy's grave. Because each of us had disclosed his thoughts in the serious meeting the previous afternoon, I knew exactly what was going on in their minds.

Eric created his own opportunity to say Kaddish for our deceased father. He was sadly looking down, avoiding eye contact with the others.
For the first time as an adult I saw him cry. Crying over a father who had never shown any compassion to him, had banned him from his life, had even tried to deny him the right to come close after his death. Irene looked at him with a caring expression of love and compassion, caressing his hand.
'Magnified and Glorified His great name…,' we started the Kaddish.

Boy and Molly were crying in each other's arms. The Kaddish took them back in time, to the worst blow in their existence, the loss of their son. After all the losses they had suffered during the Holocaust it felt to them as if there was no justice in the world.
'We didn't deserve this,' I heard Boy whisper to his wife, with a broken voice.

Fred was praying. The words were meant to be for Daisy. His thoughts were with his father. How he had bluffed himself in agony of death into the office of an SS-commander while all of his fellows in hiding were arrested, deported and killed.

Michael stood petrified, thinking about his ongoing nightmares, the dreams in which booted soldiers came to take his family away. Nightly horrors of a man who was born seven years after the war. His thoughts were with his paranoid parents too, who constantly feared that everything they owned would be stolen.

Sally had never looked so sad. She was mourning over her little brother who died of bone cancer, before he was given the opportunity to enjoy a single minute of his life without sorrow.

Phil was clinging on to Joan's arm, thinking about his chaotic mother, a father that he had never known. The way his life had indirectly been ruined by criminals who had never faced him eye to eye. Who most likely had never stood trial for their atrocities, for the cruel manner of slaughtering his family. He was hoping, begging, that his soon to come marriage with Joan would provide him with the happiness he'd never known.

Esther looked emotionless. Her mind was with her father who was physically and emotionally mutilated as a result of the dreadful circumstances, as a slave laborer at the feared Burma railroad. And with her mother and the other women who had been beaten and raped in front of her eyes in a Japanese concentration camp. Her brother who took his own life due to his suffering.

Rachel was the only one who looked angry. Anger about the kidnapping of her two children who now lived in a strict fundamentalist regime in Hebron. There was an expression of animosity when she looked at the rabbi. She supportively glanced at me with her loving eyes.

Mony was biting his lip, again trying in vain to cry about the cruelty of the medical experiments performed on his parents, the suicide of his mother, the faith of his little sister who couldn't accept his love; the loss of his grandchild, taken away from him by a fraudulent young Dutch woman; his inability to really cry or laugh.

Max was leaning his head on David's shoulder, pondering over his feelings of loneliness. The inability to explain this to his wife who loved him dearly, or to his son David. David stroked his father's hair in an attempt to comfort him.

'It's okay dad,' he whispered. 'It's going to be all right.'

Dave was praying with his eyes covered by his hand, the other one holding on to Leslie. In his head was an engraved image of his father with the Auschwitz registration number on his arm. How he used to sit on the toilet crying in the dark, telling us, 'You wouldn't understand.'

I was praying for Daisy, but my mind wandered off to thoughts about my mother's little brother who had been kicked down the stairs by the boots of a rude Amsterdam policeman. My uncle Sammy whom I had never known. The verbal and physical abuse from my parents, destroying Eric and my childhood. My father's awful reprehensible, angry, hateful expression when he looked at me for the last time from his deathbed. While the others completed the Kaddish I begged, 'Daisy, for God's sake come back. Daisy.'

I wanted to scream for her. Instead I rejoined my *Partners in Crime*, completing the Kaddish prayer.

'He who makes peace in His heights may He make peace upon us and upon all Israel,' I muttered. 'Amen.'

'Amen,' the others repeated. I looked at them. My *Partners in Crime* holding on to each other. We were not alone.

About this book

At the end of 1989 the Berlin wall collapsed. After the reunion of East and West Germany - on October 3rd, 1990 - expropriated properties by the DDR regime could be reclaimed. Furthermore, East German possessions confiscated by the Nazis between 1933 and 1945 became subject to compensation. The possessions ranged from movables, estates and works of art to factories, capital stock and bank accounts. The deadline for filing claims was December 31st, 1992.

At the time I lived in Los Angeles. In August of 1992 a friend visited me, Ingo Leetsch, an attorney who practices law in Bremen, Germany. As a non-Jewish German, born after WWII, he was most upset that the German government had provided insufficient publicity to the new ruling. The German government denied this. We decided to place a few small ads in the Jewish weeklies of greater Los Angeles. We simply offered to file claims, free of charge. People were invited to call me at home. I faxed my reports to Leetsch in Bremen, who filed the claims with the German Government. The press learned about it and soon articles appeared in over seven hundred publications throughout the United States.

During several months I received more than twelve hundred phone calls from Holocaust survivors and their children. Mostly lengthy monologues of which I made notes that became written interviews. Often the conversations were unrelated to the issue. On many occasions someone wanted to talk to a complete stranger who understood! All of these personal, touching and candid witness statements and memories were verified. During that process I discovered several shocking facts that had never been widely publicized.

After the project was finalized I found myself in the possession of a treasure of information, especially about the post-war generation. I felt the need to make these stories accessible to a larger audience, especially to youngsters; the adults of the future. In Holland and Belgium the previous edition of *Broken on the inside The War Never Ended* had already found its way to into bookstores and - most importantly - high-schools and colleges. We all have the right to know about the psychological aftermath of Hitler's genocide, which may never be forgotten. After publication of the Dutch version of this book I received reactions from all over the world. Readers provided me with additional information that I used in this book. A woman born after the war told me that she had purchased 25 copies. She gave them to friends and relatives to explain emotions that she was unable to express herself. Parts of the book have been used in scientific lectures and studies by psychologists, psychiatrists and social workers at international professional conventions.

It is beyond belief that many Holocaust survivors received a heartless reception after the war and many of them live in deep poverty. A Palm Springs resident said: "I went through hell three times. First in Auschwitz, secondly after the war when I discovered that my entire family had been murdered and now I am unskilled and penniless." Therefore I urge "the powers that be" to assume the utmost urgency and consideration in helping to minimize the suffering of those who survived, before it is too late. They deserve it. Amongst them are innocent German victims of the circumstances and – last but not least – the almost forgotten former prisoners of Japanese concentration camps.

I salute Ingo Leetsch, the late Los Angeles based clinical psychologist Florabel Kinsler and psychiatrist Marjorie Braude for their analytical research while writing this book and for the professional help they provided to war victims. And all those that had the courage to share their most intimate memories with me, so that I could write this book for future generations.

Simon Hammelburg, September 2014

The March of the Deceased was written by the author of this book.

List of Hebrew and Yiddish words

Bar Mitzvah   The ceremony in a synagogue, in which a Jewish boy at age thirteen reaches the status of an adult and is obliged to pray. The Saturday when he delivers his first prayer of thanks/blessing (bracha) is celebrated by family and friends.
Bracha   Prayer of thanks or blessing.
Chanukah   Holiday to commemorate the victory of the Jewish Maccabees over Greek despots, 165 B.C. and the restoration of the destroyed temple in Jerusalem.
Chanukiah   Eight armed candelabrum used during the eight days of Chanukah. During the eight days of Chanukah candles are lit, each day one more.
Chupah   Wedding.
Chutzpah   Impudence.
Gefilte Fish   Fish loaf made of chopped fish (preferably carp), eggs, onions, pepper and sugar.
Goy   Gentile; not Jewish.
Goyim   Non Jews.
Habonim   International socialist Jewish youth movement. Literary: The builders.
Kaddish   The Mourner's Prayer.
Kiddush Cup   Wine cup (usually silver) used during a psalm of praise of the consecration of the Sabbath and most Jewish holidays.
Kreplach   Dumpling made of chopped meat or cheese.
L'chayim   Cheers; to life.
Minyan   The ten male Jews required for a religious service.

Mikva	Ritual bath.
Mitzvah	Commandment, ethical deed or obligation.
Nebech	Poor (unfortunate) person.
Nudnick	A pest, nag, annoyer, bore.
Payess	Unshorn sideburn-locks worn by ultra-Orthodox Jewish men.
Shadchen	Matchmaker.
Shikker	Drunk.
Shul	Synagogue.
Sheitel	Wig, worn by orthodox married Jewish women.
Shiva	Seven solemn days of mourning for the dead, beginning immediately after the funeral.
Shlemiel	Foolish person, someone who has bad luck.
Shlemazel	A born looser.
Shtuss	Nonsense.
Talmud	Commentaries of scholars and jurists, interpretations of the Torah, the first five books of the Bible and teachings of ethical questions in daily life.
Touchis	Rear end.
Tsoris	Troubles.
WIZO	Women International Zionist Organization.